Biology Boy Love

Rachel Anne Jones

BIOLOGY BOY LOVE
Copyright © 2025 by Rachel Anne Jones

ISBN: 979-8-88653-417-7

Fire & Ice Young Adult Books
An Imprint of Melange Books, LLC
White Bear Lake, MN 55110
www.fireandiceya.com

Published in the United States of America.

Cover Design by Ashley Redbird Designs

"I just want you to know that you are very special...

And the only reason I'm telling you is that I don't know if anyone else ever has."

— *THE PERKS OF BEING A WALLFLOWER*

ONE

Charlie

Sam Birk sits beside me on the bleachers, lounging. His brown hair falls over his perfect brow. It's been shaped by Zeus, as my boy crazy little sister would say, and has said many, many times. She's not boy crazy so much as Sam crazy. It's a fact as unpleasant as the side effects of having an eidetic memory, which allows me to recall someone's words verbatim, no matter how asinine they may be. This particular part of my personality, paired with having a sister who salivates over my best friend on a daily basis while covering it up in a snarky tone, has me regarding his physical attributes in a whole new light. Her words crowd my cranium, and I cannot shove them out. It's highly annoying.

Sam's bottom lip juts out as he blows the offending strands from their resting place, only to have them fall back again. The sun shines on his face, giving him that *golden boy* glow, but he doesn't break a sweat. I cannot say the same for my armpits. I should not have worn a sweater-vest, even though they're my favorite. His blue eyes shine bright as he ogles the girls on the field. They jump up and down to the music, clapping their hands. I glance out at what holds his attention. Girls in tight sweaters wearing short skirts. I suppose I understand.

Maybe I could find one of them remotely attractive if my concentration wasn't ruined by the dark-haired girl in the second row clapping offbeat. I hate that I notice her accidental imperfection, as I myself have no rhythm. Now that I've noticed this dysrhythmic flaw in their synchronized dance, I can't un-notice it.

"She's so hot," he swoons.

"Who?"

He throws his head back and guffaws like the whole world agrees with him. At our high school (otherwise known as an unbalanced ecosystem of torture, one in which my best friend, Sam Birk, is the top of the food chain) everyone does indeed guffaw with him.

"Exactly," he crows as he reaches out and pats my shoulder a little too hard. "You got it, Charlie. They're all hot. I would hook up with any of 'em." As usual, Sam gives me far too much credit for understanding the way his oversexed brain operates. He can't help himself. He understands what everyone wants to hear – all the time. He can't stop himself from being the handsome Prince of Seeberger High.

His misogynistic words burn my virgin ears. I hate how any sort of interaction with the opposite sex renders me clumsy and slow, like I'm wading through muddy pond bottoms in flip-flops and not my highly-recommended waders I received last May. That delivery was by way of USPS, the slowest system on the planet, when one is waiting for something with the same degree of anticipation a preschooler waits for Santa Claus to come down the chimney on Christmas Eve. It is my lifelong dream to become a marine biologist and someday I will achieve that dream. I will look back on every miserable second of my life at Seeberger High with a sardonic smile, because it will all be in my rearview mirror. At least that's what Mom promises me every day while shoving me out the front door. Dad gives me a wink and a smile, telling me to look for silver linings. Yet clouds never interested me, and ponds and lakes have no silver linings.

Speaking of bodies of water (one of my favorite subjects), last summer my helicopter mother finally relinquished her hold on me and allowed me to go to nerd camp for future marine biologists. At least that's what my sister called it, but I was too excited to care. She can call it whatever she likes, so long as I get to go to my happy place. That's where it's cool to search for that unknown discovery in nature waiting for me.

"She is so fine," Sam murmurs, jolting me back to reality. The thing about Sam that I find so interesting is that every time he talks about a girl, he pretends he's never uttered those same words about another girl just days or weeks before. Mom claims he has an addiction to infatuation. I think she's right. Mom's really good at getting people, including me, her quiet, introverted son with a terrible case of tunnel vision that's plagued me since I was seven years old. That was the day I saw my first clown fish.

"Haven't you already," I joke (sort of) as I wave toward the group of girls. "Like haven't you already, you know..." my voice drops off. Why do I have to be so awkward? "Like with all of them?"

Sam squeezes my shoulder just hard enough to remind me which one of us is the starting quarterback on Varsity for the third year in a row. "Only half," he replies. Then he relaxes his grip, leans forward to rest his elbows on his knees and flexes his biceps.

My sister's latest complaint about Sam from the other morning rings in my ears. "Sam Birk acts like he's in a commercial or on TikTok all the time. He's so used to people looking at him, he can't turn it off." As much as I hate to admit it, I'm going to miss her nurturing ways when I go off to college. What I'm not going to miss is her constant drooling over Sam Birk, but I deal with it if it means free food.

Her latest Sam Birk complaint/observation confused me at the time, but that's nothing new. My sister Creed never shuts up about Sam, and only half of what she says makes any sense. We get along alright; but if we weren't related, we would not be considered the same species. Once we leave home and go our separate ways, she has her world, and I have mine.

"Turn what off?" I asked as I focused on my charcoal drawing in my sketchpad.

She shoved me. It messed with my drawing and pissed me off. I laid down my graphite and got to work with my kneaded eraser.

"Dude. You messed up my operculum." I gave her serious side-eye.

"Don't irritate me when you're drawing, nerd boy," she teased, "and I won't mess with your Oppenheimer." For half a second, I was even madder than before. I thought she wasn't going to answer my question. I hate it when she does that, just like I hate it when she says the wrong words on purpose just to rile me. She knows how much it bothers me to not have something answered, but she never leaves me hanging when it comes to her thoughts on Sam Birk, the hottest boy at Seeberger High. Again, those are her words. Not mine. The only thing lamer than the name of our high school is our mascot. We're the Seeberger High Sea Lions.

"Sam Birk lives his life like he has his own reality show," she continued.

I guess some guys would be jealous if their best friend was as popular as mine, but I don't care. Sometimes I wonder why he continues to hang out with me, the guy whose one goal is to not be in a single yearbook photograph.

The one benefit about attending a 5A high school is the variety of advanced academic courses available to the student body. The amount of focus required for every touchdown Sam scored on the football field and every pin he made on the wrestling mats is the same amount I give to taking every weighted class that rests across the road from the biggest outdoor sculpture park in the tristate area, which does wonders for its otherwise lameass location according to my linguistically-challenged sister. My sister, who has the attention span of phytoplankton, loves to attach the word "ass" to as many words as possible.

My desires are a little more complicated than hers. I long to explore the vastness of the ocean and to discover an unknown species in its abyssal depths. I can't logically explain my love of the water and what lies below. I only know my infatuation with ecosystems will never change.

I can still recall the exact moment it hit me. I was seven years old, and I *knew* from the moment I set foot in the giant aquarium house at the amusement park that I would never see anything as fascinating as all the colorful fish behind the glass floating back and forth. Their eyes were wide open, unfocused and unblinking. I wanted to know what they perceived. I wanted to see the world through their weird, bugged-out eyes. But more than that, I needed an explanation for the existence of the most beautiful and weird creatures I'd ever laid eyes upon. I needed to understand where they came from.

As I stood there mesmerized, I asked myself if they could see me as I did in my reflection: a scrawny boy in his favorite red and white striped shirt, dirty blue jeans, and messy hair with his hands pressed to the glass, staring in awe and wonder. My dream in that moment felt so real. If only my hands could reach through the glass and touch the paper-thin fin fluttering as fast as my heartbeat, it would have slowed the heaving of my chest. My insides were so big they had to come out.

It must have been too much for my mother to take, for she grabbed my upper arm and tugged me away from the fat, round glass pillar that shot straight up to a ceiling so high it went to infinity and beyond. My mind was dizzy with unanswered questions that couldn't reach my lips. How did the fish get in there? Who fed them and how? Were they going to go back to where they came from? And where was that? As I stood there drooling, Mom teased, "Charlie. Look somewhere else before you hyperventilate." I could make out the alarm in her voice and her pinch.

"I'm sorry," I answered. She accepted my afterthought of an offering, even though my understanding of the apology and hers slightly differed. Fortunately for me, Dad's one and only regret was standing between me and the great waters. While I glanced up at the banners, imagining myself as one of the scuba divers depicted, Dad released premature dreams of fields of grass with sandbags strewn here and there. They made up fond childhood memories he had hoped to share with me.

Dad is not one to complain, but there were a few times when I caught him staring out the car window with longing at a nearby stadium. He would act like a man caught cheating by ducking or changing the song on the radio before clearing his throat as if to say, "Well, that's that. Moving on."

So here on the bleachers, Sam basks in the sun while I roam the hallways of my short life. Our class just picked out our graduation gown colors. That must be what has me nostalgic as I take another stroll down memory lane. I glance over at Sam, who haphazardly watches Keersten's barely-there skirt that flaps up now and then.

He peeks at her silver sparkly booty shorts while she pretends she doesn't notice because she's too busy perfecting her flyer pose and balancing on the palm of Kyle's large, capable hand. I slap Sam's knee. "Dude. You're not even trying."

He flashes me his signature grin. "Yeah, I know. Marzipan told me last week Keersten has a crush on me. She totally got inside my head."

I glance at Keersten and back at Sam. "You're so easy, it's ridic —" And that's when I spot a girl in the corner of my eye. She comes around the side of the bleachers. She's an unexpected interruption to my frustrating, suffocating life. Ever since I picked out my graduation gown, I go backward and forward at the same time. I don't want to be in either of those places, but none of that matters. Not at this moment.

I take in the most beautiful human I've ever laid eyes on. There was the time before I saw her, and there is now. This has to be the best day ever. I'm electrified. Every nerve in my body is on high alert. I want to get up from where I'm sitting and go to her as she stands next to Creed, whose eyes are glued to the side of Sam's face. Sam can't turn his head when his eyeballs are affixed to Keersten's glittery booty shorts as she stretches for the fiftieth time in the span of thirty-seven minutes. My eyes are rolling in my head. All I want is to watch this girl for as much and as long as possible. I wish Sam and Creed would disappear.

Creed jerks her head sideways to catch what holds Sam's undivided attention. "*Gross,*" she snorts. "What does she think she's doing, acting like she's in some sort of shady music video with her butt in the air? And here I thought her face was the only part of her that's utterly repulsive."

Sam laughs beside me. "That's your opinion, Creed."

I should look down. The pain in Creed's face at Sam's not-so-subtle drooling over Keersten's is so obvious. But I can't stop staring at the girl who stands next to Creed, not even when Creed glares at me. "So, anyway. This is Venus Moon. She's new here. I'm showing her around."

"But the school year's already started," I blurt.

Venus stares at me with her green eyes. I grip the side of the bleachers to be sure I'm not falling. I recall the time I pulled into the parking space at the same time someone backed out. I was so sure I was going to hit the curb at any second that a sense of panic came over me, I looked down to be sure my feet weren't on the gas pedals. It was the most disconcerting feeling I've ever had. Until now. It's as if my vestibular system has been disrupted and my equilibrium has gone haywire. I'm in a constant state of falling.

"Her mom took a job at the hospital. She's in administration," Creed announces, but I barely listen. I can't stop staring, so I force myself to focus on a button on Venus's backpack.

"The Mourning Doves," I mutter at the same time she covers it.

"Don't mind my brother. He's socially challenged," Creed comments like she has so many times before. And it's never bothered me because I mostly concur. But it bothers me now. The very thought that this girl would see any weakness in me is too much.

"My name is Charlie," I blurt as Creed's still talking. Or she was. She stops midsentence. Her blue eyes bug, but Venus just smiles at me like she has all the patience in the world.

She extends her hand. I'm swimming against the tide as I release my white-knuckled grip on the bleacher to move toward her. It's a movement that is perfectly normal, an everyday occurrence in her world, I'm sure. But not for me. Her hand is like sunshine in my palm. I want to hold onto it forever.

"There," she chirps. "Now we've properly met."

Creed wrinkles her nose. "Barf. Stop holding my brother's hand," she whines.

Venus lets go of me. I'm devastated. I hate my sister. I wish she would fall to the ground in a seizure. Anything to make her stop humiliating me in front of the most perfect girl. I blink. *I take it back. I don't want my sister to get sick. I am a terrible person. What is going on?* "I didn't mean it," I mutter.

Creed rolls her eyes. "Mean what, Charlie? What are you *talking about?*"

I'm so relieved my seizure-inducing thoughts for my sister stayed inside my head. "Nothing."

Sam is on his feet. He hops over two rows of bleachers like he's a South African sharp-nosed frog. He smiles at Venus, giving her his full attention. *I want to punch him in the face.* I glance at Creed. By the way she glares, she agrees with me for once.

"What's up? I'm Sam." He points to the button on her bag as if he knows everything on the subject. "So you like the Mourning Doves, I see." I've seen Sam do this so many times. He subtly takes credit for something someone else noticed first or whatever. I've never cared before, but now I do.

I hate that I'm waiting for her answer on baited breath.

"Yeah. I do," she replies. "How about you? What do you think of them?"

Sam's smile shrinks. "Oh, I don't know." I feel an insult coming. When Sam is insecure, which is somewhere in the time frame between never and ever, he insults the girl to knock her down a few pegs. I've seen it happen a few times. "They might have had one song that could've been a hit, but it just couldn't quite get there, you know." He gives her his ingratiating smile that takes girls out at the knees.

Venus smiles back at him, but there's something in her smile. She has a secret. Is this really happening? Does a girl exist who is immune to Sam's charms? What does this mean? My sinking heart starts to bob.

"Yeah, maybe," she replies, but her answer doesn't ring quite true. She's not fully committed to it. She's just being nice. I make a mental note to google Mourning Doves as soon as possible. My fingers itch to do it right now, but I won't. Creed told me it's impolite to fact-check people in the middle of a conversation. It's not that I want to fact-check my best friend, even if he's trying to impress the one girl I've ever been remotely interested in, and I think he knows. *I mean, how could he not know?* Human contact is my least favorite activity, and I just shook her hand. He knows I go out of my way not to touch people's skin, just like he knows I rarely go out of my way to speak to strangers.

"Well. This has all been very illuminating, but Venus and I have to keep moving. We have better things to do than stand around talking to you two pervs," Creed challenges while staring Sam down.

He gives her a wink and an even bigger smile. "If I didn't know better, I'd say someone's jealous."

Creed's cheeks turn pink. "Yeah, right. Like I would be jealous of a girl who made up a song just so she can remember how to spell awesome," she sneers before slipping her hand through Venus's elbow. "Come on. Let's go." I have to admit, my sister is pretty creative with her snark.

TWO

Venus

"So now you've met the biggest player at Seeberger High," Creed grumbles to me. Her words are meant to be insulting, but I hear the admiration in her voice.

"Your brother," I reply in the most earnest tone I can manage.

She halts as we head up the small hill that leads to the side of the high school. "Um, no. I'm talking about *Sam Birk*, the starting quarterback for the football team. He's made the all-star team three years in a row, and he's gone to state in wrestling every year. If he goes this year, he'll be like the first student to like ever do it."

I dig my elbow in her ribs just a little. "Chillax, girl. I was *kidding*. I'm not that dense. It's obvs your brother is not Mister Popularity."

She tenses beside me. "We can't all be like Sam Birk," she murmurs. I feel bad.

"Hey. I was just making an observation. I didn't mean anything by it." I clear my throat. "So what was up with your brother? He seemed a little nervous."

She wrinkles her nose again. I like this girl. Her facial expressions are hilarious. "*Did he*? I guess I didn't notice. I was *kind of* distracted."

"By the hottie QB?"

She giggles. "Maybe." She sighs. "The guy's got serious game. On and off the field. He'll never notice me."

I grab her upper arm. "That's not true. You just have to be patient, and you have to be ready."

Her eyes widen. She stares at me with so much hope, I don't want to disappoint her. "Really?"

I exhale slowly. "I can't make any promises, but I can tell you this. If you want something, you have to go after it. You can't wait for it to come to you. In my experience, the 'sitting around and waiting to be noticed' method doesn't get the best results."

She smiles once more. "You're practical. I like that. My brother doesn't mean to be so awkward. It's just that he has tunnel vision. He wants to be a marine biologist someday. He's extremely focused. He doesn't really see any reason to spend time doing things that do not pertain to that goal."

We start walking again.

"So he likes looking at plant life?" I ask.

She nods. "Anything that lives and breathes in the water, yes."

"So he could be like a person who studies sharks."

She giggles again. "Technically, yes. I suppose he could, but that's really Charlie's style. He tends to avoid anything scary or threatening." She smirks a little. "He won't even watch horror movies with me. They give him nightmares."

I shrug. "That's okay. They're unimaginative."

She shoves me so hard I almost fall off the sidewalk into the grass. "Shut up. Horror movies are not unimaginative. *How dare you.*"

I rub the side of my arm she shoved. She's stronger than she looks. "I'm sorry, but I stand by my original opinion. All they do is show how many different ways a person can bleed out and die. And who leaves their vehicle on the side of the road and walks into a dark house in a remote setting on the night of a full moon? It's so cliché."

She waves her jazz hands in front of my face. "Okay, okay already. Agree to disagree. How about that?"

I probably shouldn't ask her more about her brother, but

there's just something about Charlie. "So that's what the shark shirt was about."

"I already told you. *Marine biology*," she drawls as if it's a dirty word. "It's been that way since he was like seven-years-old." My ears burn. I can't imagine being that sure about anything. "For real?"

She nods. "Yeah. For real." She looks over at me. "It's weird, right?"

She opens the side door. We walk into the gym. "I don't know. I think it'd be nice to be that committed to something. Sometimes I wish someone would just tell me what I'm going to do with the rest of my life."

She goes to shove me again. This time I see it coming, and I dodge. She half stumbles to the floor before she catches herself. I tense up for half a second. I hope I didn't enrage her. She plops down on her butt before glancing up at me. "I didn't expect you to move."

"I don't like being shoved," I remind her as gently as possible.

"Noted," she replies before sticking out her hand. "Give me a hand up?"

I high-five her. "I don't quite trust you. I have to get to my locker." I jog through the door and slip into the crowded hallway of students bumping into each other like drunk ping-pong balls. The crowded chaos relaxes me. It's as welcoming as a beautiful bouquet of flowers I can disappear into, until someone plucks me. Judging by my how my day has gone so far, Seeberger High apparently still believes in the ancient practice of polite society. If I have to stand up and tell a classroom full of total strangers one more time something about myself, I think I'll scream.

I walk through the door of Mrs. Hernandez, who teaches Spanish III. "Hola," she chirps. "Me llamo Senora Hernandez."

"Hola," I respond. "Me gusto su jaqueta azul y verdes."

"Gracias. Es de Mexico."

I nod before sitting down in the second row. "Es muy bien," I agree. "Mi padre viva en Mexico,." Then I scan the room. I can't believe I just said that. It's the truth, but I don't usually talk about it.

If my teacher is surprised by my answer, she hides it well. "Es muy interesante."

"Si," a boy chimes in as he sneaks into the room.

"Charlie?" Mrs. Hernandez gasps.

"Que," he replies confidently, but I spy the tremor in his hand as he taps the side of his leg. What is going on?

"What are you doing here?"

"Soy estudiante," he jokes, kind of, but I hear something else in his tone. Determination.

"Esta es una mala hora," she answers.

He's on his phone. Is he ignoring her? "No. Esta es la hora equivocada," he rattles off as he reads his phone. Then he slides into the desk next to mine.

Her hand is out. "Dame su telefono."

He grabs his phone by the one edge and waits. "Esta aqui."

I glance around as I try to ignore him staring at me. Somehow the room filled up during their short conversation. I think he's supposed to be somewhere else, but he's here. And I suspect it's because of me. But that can't be. We just met. I've never had a stalker. That's what he would be, right? But I don't think this is about me. I'm not that special, and he doesn't seem like the creepy type. If anything, he appears to be confused as I study him out of the corner of my eye. Mrs. Hernandez snatches her end of his phone and pries it from his grasp before walking to the other side of her desk. She claps her hands. "Okay, everyone partner up and continue on your projects." Her gaze returns to me and Charlie. "You two step outside in the hallway with me."

This isn't ideal, but it's better than the first and second hour when I had to stand up in the middle of the room and tell everyone my name, where I moved from, and something special about myself. The only thing special about me is how many times I've moved in my short life. I follow Mrs. Hernandez out of the room while managing to mostly ignore Charlie, who gives me my space. He closes the door behind him.

"Charlie," she begins, but she doesn't sound mad. "Where are you supposed to be right now?"

"In this building," he replies.

She rolls her eyes. I think I like her. "Charlie. I know you're a senior and you've taken every possible weighted class there is to take, but boredom is not a reason to start causing trouble. I'm going to ask you again. Where are you supposed to be right now?"

"In Mr. J's A&P class," he answers while he stares at something behind Mrs. Hernandez's right shoulder.

"And you just decided to *ditch* Mr. J's class today so you can come and sit in my room?" she demands. "Did you at least tell him?"

"No," he replies unapologetically. "I suppose I should have."

"If you don't want your parents getting a letter of warning, yeah," she retorts.

"Why would my parents receive that letter? I'm almost eighteen."

"Charlie. Your parents are legally responsible for you. You know how this state operates. If a student is absent or tardy too many days, the parent is notified. If the behavior continues, the parents are fined."

His eyes widen. "Are you telling me if I skip school my parents have to pay the school?"

She nods. "Yes. That is correct."

"How is that fair?" he demands.

She waves between us. "I don't make the rules, Charlie. Okay? I just follow them. So whatever your reason is for transferring to my classroom this far into the school year," she continues pointedly while staring me down, "it had better be a good one. Will you at least tell Mr. Johnson why you chose to miss his class today?"

"Fine. I'll tell him something."

She crosses her arms. "So you're not going to tell me why you decided to come in here this far into the semester."

He shoves his hands in his cargo pants pockets. He has a pained look on his face. "We aren't that far in, and I don't know. I guess I felt like a change," he mutters while looking off to the side.

She taps her toe. "A *change*. Well, that's just fine and dandy. I mean, what if the rest of the students decided to switch classes midsemester. Do you know what sort of mess that would make?"

He scratches the back of his neck with one hand while returning his gaze to his teacher. "Muy grande," he replies with a small grin. I'm so glad he's looking at Mrs. Hernandez and not me. The boy has awkward charm, and it's freaking adorable. He's totally unaware.

Her dark curls slide along her cheek when she ducks her chin in agreement. "That's right, Charlie. A big one. If I let you in my classroom, how do I know you won't leave two weeks from now?"

His head cocks to the side just a little. A mole peeks out at me from the underside of his chin. "I won't do that. I promise." He leans back on his heels. His one hand is still in his pocket. "I don't need A&P, Mrs. Hernandez. I really feel taking this class will benefit me more in the long run."

She stares him down. "Since when did a marine biologist need to know a second language?"

His green eyes widen. I never knew I loved green eyes so much. I mean, I have green eyes but they're nothing like Charlie's. His have just enough blue in them they remind me of the ocean. "I don't understand why you aren't happy with me taking your class. You've been wanting me to take it since last year."

Her hands fly this way and that. "Fine. I'll let you in, but it's mostly because I don't want the headache of trying to work Venus here into another group. It wouldn't be fair to the others for her to get credit when she just got here." She reaches into her messenger bag and pulls out two pieces of paper. "Read over this. It outlines the project details. You two are starting out two weeks behind, which means you're going to have to put some serious work in to catch up. I won't have you holding everyone else back because you're on your own schedules," she warns. Her initial friendliness has all but disappeared.

A moment of panic sets in as I comprehend what just happened. I'm in a group project with the boy who gives me all the feels. But it's not really a group. There's just two of us, so it's more like a partnership. How am I going to hide my feelings from him, and what if I can't? I just made a really good friend with his sister. She's not going to want me drooling over her brother. I need some distance.

We can't do this project together. He's so smart. Even though we just met, there's something about him I can't explain. I don't know if it's the fact that he's like this quirky brainiac that has me dazed or that he's acting like a possessive movie vampire who has to be near me, because why else would he transfer into a classroom on the day we met? It might make me like super self-centered, but it's true. I've never felt so interesting in all my life. Up until now the only thing significant about me is that my best friend has a crush on the hottest, sluttiest guy at Seeberger High, who flirted with me.

I'm not stupid. I know it's because I'm new. I'm fresh meat and all that, which by the way is a term I absolutely abhor. It makes it sound like teenage boys are a pack of wild wolves that never bathe.

I study Charlie once more out of the corner of my eye. I think he was flirting with me, but I'm not entirely sure. I suppose it could be a huge coincidence that he wants to take Spanish III, and that he made this decision the day he met me. He's totally not looking at me as he flips a guitar pick over and over between his fingers. I can't believe he plays the guitar. That's so hot.

I glance back at my new teacher. I raise my hand to the level of my shoulder. "Excuse me."

"Yes?"

"I don't know that I want to be his partner," I squeak while trying to avoid looking at green-eyed Charlie. He's tall, in my personal space, totally watching, and impossible to ignore unless I completely turn my back on him.

"Excuse me," he interrupts. "I think I've made a mistake. I'll just go somewhere else." Charlie strides to the nearest corner before taking an abrupt turn and disappearing from my sight.

Mrs. Hernandez turns back to me. Her brown eyes harden. I wish I didn't like her eye makeup so much.

"Why is it that you don't want to be his partner? Did he do something offensive? Did he insult you in any way?" she asks. This is so annoying. Why can't she just lose her shit over something so mundane as me leaving the room to pee like my last Spanish teacher did at my old school? I force myself to refocus. Mrs. Hernandez waits for an answer. She's slightly irritated, but she's way too rational. I'm such an idiot.

"No. It's just that. Well, I don't know how well we're going to get along is all," I offer. I can't think of any other excuse. I don't really want to tell her that I'm not sure how I feel about him. I don't want him to know I feel academically and linguistically challenged whenever I think of speaking in front of him. There's also the strange unexplainable feeling that I want to be alone with him, but I don't, because I don't trust my feelings. I'm not up for having that discussion with anyone.

Her friendly smile disappears. "I know Charlie. He's a little quiet, but he's a good student. He'll take this project seriously. I hope you will do the same. So unless you feel unsafe or threatened in his presence, I see no reason for you to not able to work with him. This assignment has always been one of my student's favorites, and you could enjoy it. Either way, it's 75-80 percent of your grade, so I suggest you get to work on it soon." Her brown eyes hold no anger, and her positive yet forceful tone is full of encouragement.

I'm an idiot. This is me overreacting to what I thought was happening when it clearly wasn't. Charlie has no interest in me. If he did, he wouldn't have taken off on me like that. He's such a brainiac. There can't be anything I could possibly teach him in any subject.

I mull over her words. "I'll work on the project, but I'm not sure I have a partner. He just took off," I protest.

She smiles at me like she knows something I don't. "Stay right here. I'll get you a library pass. I'm pretty sure that's where he went, just like I'm pretty sure *you* can convince him to come back to class."

Just thinking about talking to him after I told her in front of

17

him I didn't want to work with him makes me feel muy estupido. I clutch the sombrero/hall pass that's twice as wide as me while I make my way to the library.

I don't see him. I walk down every book aisle and try to pretend the reason everyone's staring at me is because I'm holding a giant red velvet sombrero with *Dead Guy Duty* scrawled across the front in curlicue gold letters, and not because I'm the new kid trying to be cool when I'm anything but. It doesn't take long to discover he's not between the shelves.

This library is not as big as it should be for the size of the school, but that's not too surprising. It's a lot like the library at my old school. Every student in the room sits in the back in front of a computer with headphones jammed in their ears. I study the backs of their heads. Maybe Mrs. Hernandez doesn't know Charlie as well as she thinks she does.

I'm about to give up when something draws me to the one corner I haven't covered. I wander over, and that's when I realize this corner has more depth. There's a nook on the other side, and there he sits. He's as still as stone with his empty stare. I step closer and closer until the two of us are behind the wall. "Hi," I begin.

"Hello," he answers, mirroring my nervousness.

"I have something to tell you," I whisper.

"So say it already," he fires back, surprising me.

I sink into the beanbag across from him, prop myself up on my elbows, and stretch out my legs until my ankles almost bump his hip. He leans against the wall, his knees drawn close to his chest. I can't bring myself to meet his gaze, so I cover my face with the big sombrero. "I want you to come back to Spanish class," I blurt from beneath my big hat.

He sits there for what feels like forever. I almost peek out to see if he heard me, but I can't. "Por qué?"

"Because I need you to be my partner."

"Por qué?"

He's so infuriating. "Dude. You know why. You were standing right there when Mrs. Hernandez told us about the project," I accuse while flinging my hands around. I can't seem to talk without moving my hands, especially when I'm annoyed.

"Silencio. Keep it down. You're going to get us kicked out of la bibiloteca," he warns.

I do not like being told what to do, especially by a guy. "Are you in or out, 'cause I kinda need to know. If I'm doing this on my own, I need to get to work. Like now."

"And if I decide to be your partner?"

I roll my eyes beneath my hat. "Dude. I'm not going to beg you. I'm only here because Mrs. H sent me down here. Either way, I've got stuff to do. I'm already almost a month behind everyone else, or did you not hear her explain that before you stomped off like a toddler?"

I shouldn't be so mean, but he was a bit ridiculous.

"I didn't stomp. I was very quiet," he retorts. "Some might even say stealth." I hate how much I like his choice of words. The boy is no dummy.

I wish I could see his face so I knew more of what he was thinking, but I'm committed to keeping the oversized hat in place. I'm the one who put it there, and to move it would be to admit I'm being ridiculous. Some questions are easier to ask when I'm not staring him dead in the eye. "Why'd you come to class after the semester already started?" I demand.

"That's not your concern."

I move my foot around until it bumps into him. "Are you like stalking me?" I tease as my face heats. I'm so glad I'm beneath the sombrero.

"No," he blubbers. I should feel bad, but I don't.

"So you didn't come in there for me?" I cross the line from accusatory to desperate. Why can't I shut up?

"Did you want me to?" he asks. It's a fair question, and the last thing I thought he'd say. I don't have an answer. At least not one I'm ready to give.

My hands still as I reach for the edge of my sombrero. "That's not what I said," I spit out. I should change the subject. Like now.

"So are we partners or what?" I ask.

"Fine. But you'd better not make me sorry I decided to be your partner. I'm doing a favor, you know," he grumbles, as if he expects me to bow down and kiss his feet.

"So you're dropping A&P? Just like that?" I don't know why I care, but he doesn't seem the type of guy to change his mind on a whim.

Part of him bumps me back. I feel the jolt all the way up to my butt. It's so weird.

"I'm not dropping A&P. I'm adding something to my schedule. I'll juggle my hours. I've done it before."

My head aches just thinking about his load. "So you live your life in books."

"Pretty much. Unless I'm at the ponds classifying species."

"But they're already classified," I argue.

"Not necessarily. In marine biology, we classify species according to the environment, which differs from using taxonomy," he explains. I'd swear he's said it like a thousand times.

"You should be a teacher," I blurt.

"I'm going to be a marine biologist," he replies irritably. "I already told you this."

"But you're so sure of yourself," I argue. Although I'm not sure of anything that includes me, I'm sure about him. He's the most confident guy I've ever met. "You'd have no trouble teaching others about science and nature."

"I'm not a people person. I do not enjoy conversing. It's not easy for me," he whispers.

I nudge him again with my foot. "You're doing just fine," I offer.

He moves away from my offending foot until I'm no longer touching him. I don't know what I expected, but it wasn't that. I shift the sombrero just enough so I can see some of him, but it still dips over my eyebrows.

"You don't know me like you think you do," he murmurs. Then he folds his knees to his chest, wraps his long arms around his knees and lays his head sideways on his one knee.

"So what would you classify me as?" I tease. My heart freezes for a split second. I can't believe how much I want to know what he's about to say.

"That's easy. You're a homo sapiens," he declares while he stares at the wall.

I giggle. I can't help it. He's so serious. "Yo soy homo sapiens," I reply in the same solemn manner. I've been told I do great imitations.

"Is everything a joke to you?" he grumps.

I straighten up. "No. Not everything." I slide the sombrero back a little farther so I can look him in the eye. "So are you going to go back to class with me or what? Senora Hernandez told me to come and get you. She said you'd be here."

"I guess she knows me," he replies, grinning with such satisfaction and gratitude I wish he was talking about me. Then he rises from the floor slowly.

I mimic his movements and wait for him to walk out. He doesn't. "Ladies first."

I step past him, giving him his space. I'm not bumping into him again just to have him avoid me like I'm a leper. I tiptoe around the wall. His hand brushes the back of my hoodie. It was so slight, it's as if I imagined it. I don't think it was a mistake, but why would he do that? I thought he didn't want me to touch him. Every atom in my body wants to stop moving and make him do it again, but fear of having no Spanish class partner moves me forward.

THREE

Charlie

I can't believe I walked into Mrs. Hernandez's class midsemester. What is wrong with me? And what am I going to tell Mr. Johnson to convince him to let me take A&P online? These thoughts trail me down the hall to his classroom. His door is closed because the bell hasn't rung. I stand outside like a creature lost in its own ecosystem. I peer through the narrow piece of glass to examine the other side of the room and one of the three students. Carlos lifts his head and stares back at me with a knowing smirk before flipping me his favorite finger.

Tiffany swings the door open and almost hits me in the face. Her platinum blonde hair (with streaks of purple) has a bunch of tiny rubber bands in it. She looks like she stuck her finger in a light socket. "What are you waiting for? Come in," she orders. "I'm going to find a tampon." Tiffany is forever making proclamations I wish I could unhear.

I walk past her. I didn't want to face Mr. J, but anything is better than hearing Tiffany commentate on routine bodily functions. I see surprise in Mr. J's eyes right before he returns to reading whatever textbook lays on his desk. He's not going to make this easy for me. I wait until I'm so close to his desk that the tips of my toes are underneath it. "I'm sorry I missed your class," I mumble.

"Umm hmmm," he answers.

"I was in Mrs. Hernandez's room. I think I'll take Spanish III."

"Umm hmmm," he answers again.

"It's just...she wanted me to, but I didn't, but now that I think about it some more, I think I should, so I guess I was just wondering if I could still take this class too. Like online."

"Umm hmmm," he repeats. It's getting on my nerves.

"So we're good then. Can I take it online?" I ask again.

His head pops up. He drops his pencil on the textbook. It rolls to the middle. "Why?"

I shift from one foot to the other. "I just told you."

He leans back in his chair. "Why can't you take *her* class online?"

I cross my arms and scour my mind for a logical answer and not the only one I can think of. *I met the most perfect girl, and I need to be near her as much as possible. I did not know a breathing apparatus existed that could help me navigate my way through this ecosystem called school that sucks me under until I met Venus. She is my lifesaver. She is the only person who makes me want to surface.* "It's Spanish. Most of the learning we do is done by speaking it out loud, so we need to be around our peers to practice pronunciation."

He stares up at me from where he sits at his desk. If I didn't know better, I'd swear he knows I'm lying. Why can't I just tell him the real reason? It's not like me to make things up. "He has a crush on the new girl, and she's in that class," loudmouth Carlos yells from the back of the room. I wish for a giant wave to roll through the room, separating us all before it drags me under. Immediately. I'm so glad the classroom door is closed. I can't imagine what I'd do if Venus heard Carlos. I wonder how long crushes last.

Mr. J blinks a few times. "Is that true?" he asks in a low voice meant only for me.

I nod. My brain is as frozen as my lips. There's nothing I can say. He scribbles across the paper. The bell rings. He tears the corner off and folds it in half. "There's my email. We'll figure something out." He gives me a wink. "Whoever she is, she's a lucky girl."

"Thank you," I manage. This whole thing is too weird.

Mr. J keeps on smiling. He's not particularly fond of smiling. "Hey. Believe it or not, I was young once. I don't envy you a bit." His smile dims and his eyes become more focused. "Just be yourself, Charlie. You'll be alright."

If only it were that easy. I'm not alright. I'm pretty sure I'll never be alright again. Half of me wishes I could follow Venus around. Forever. The other half wants to return to the normalcy of wishing for graduation day, college, and bodies of water. Studying plant and animal life. That's all I've ever wanted. But now there's this girl. And she's taking up more time and space in my brain than I am comfortable with. But graduation is just months away. So if I can avoid her until that time, and then go away to college, time and space will be between us and I will stop thinking about her. My chest aches. My breathing strains. I solved my problem in my head, so why do I feel worse instead of better? I need to go to the nurse's office.

"Charlie. Are you alright?" Mr. J asks.

I nod. I can't form words. I stumble through the desks and into the hallway. I hug the wall all the way to the nurse's office. I hate going there, but I'm going to fall over. Touching the nurse's doorknob makes me cringe. Who knows how many sick hands with germy fingers have wrapped themselves around the knob to pull the super heavy door open like I do before I flop down on the long bench and stare at the ceiling while reaching for the hand sanitizer. I turn my head before I accidentally squirt myself in the eye.

"Mrs. Gorse?" It's so strange calling her Mrs. Gorse. I've known her like most of my life. My mother and her are close friends. This is the only reason I was subjected to boardgame night with her son Printz every week for like four years until I figured out I could pay him five bucks to let me crawl out his bedroom window to sit on his roof in silence. It was my week's allowance, but it was always worth it. I never understood why everyone loves playing Monopoly. It's not even real.

"Charlie? What are you doing here?" Cindy asks.

"I just need to calm down," I answer.

She giggles. I wasn't trying to be funny.

"Would you like a drink of water?" she offers.

Sure. If that will make you go away. "No. Thank you. I think I'm fine. I'm just working some things out," I reply. I'm sure I sound strange, but I don't like lying. I just don't know what to say. I'm not talking to Mrs. Gorse about a girl.

A girl I don't know pops her head inside the room. She glances at me and then at Cindy. "Hey. Do you have a tampon? The girl's bathroom is out."

I close my eyes and resist the urge to plug my ears. Why is every girl on their menstrual cycle at the same time? And why do they have to be so vocal about it?

"Sure, Sarah. Just a minute," Cindy answers before her footsteps quiet.

"Why are you here?" Sarah demands. She must be talking to me.

I open one eye and study her while I try to formulate an answer. She's probably cute. I don't know. Her hair is long and shiny. Her lips are shiny too. She has a symmetrical face. She's wearing a shirt that doesn't cover her stomach and tight pants. She seems like the kind of girl Sam would be into. "That's not really your concern," I answer.

She wrinkles her nose at me. "Excuse me?"

I think she's annoyed. I'm not sure. "Okay." She pulls gum out of her mouth and wraps it around her finger. It's kind of gross. "You're not supposed to have gum," I tell her.

She rolls her eyes before they widen. "Hey. You were with Sam today. I saw you sitting by him on the bleachers." She tilts her head to the side. "Are you like his tutor or something?"

I'm so confused. He's never had trouble in his classes. "No. We're friends."

"Yeah, right," she snickers.

"We are. I could give you his number some time. Like maybe at the end of next week," I offer.

She tilts her head to the other side and pulls on the gum some more. "Why next week? Why not now?"

My confusion grows. I may not know much about girls, but even I know how the reproductive system works. "Most girls call him to hook up, and you came in here for a tampon."

"Charlie," Cindy calls, startling me. I turn to her. She's frowning.

"Yeah."

"You seem fine to me. You may go now."

I sit up from where I lay on the bench before I get to my feet to walk by the tampon girl. I make a mental note of the button on her backpack as I walk by that reads "Polyamory is for quitters." Sam always says I don't pay attention when he asks me about the girls who asked about him. It happens a lot, but it's hard to pay attention when I don't find them interesting. Her button is interesting.

I slide into the desk next to Sam's in the only class we have together - government. "A girl asked about you," I tell him. "But she's on her period."

The guy behind us starts laughing. "Sucks for you, bro." I'm not sure who he's talking to.

Sam whips around at his desk and punches the guy in the leg. The guy makes a face, rubs his leg, and sticks out his middle finger. Sam whips back around. "So who was she?"

I shrug. "I don't know. I met her in the nurse's office. Her backpack has a button on it. It says, 'Polyamory is for quitters.'"

He looks at me like I'm crazy. "For real?"

I nod. "I'm not making it up. That's what it said. I told her I'd give her your number next week."

He shakes his head. "Do I wanna know why?"

What is going on? Why am I the only one who understands my decisions? "She asked for a tampon," I tell him. "Because she's on her period."

"And?"

I'm so done talking about this subject. Why won't Mr. Bell yell at us? He's like totally on his phone. "She can't hook up with you if she's on her period. Why else would she be calling you?"

The guy behind me kicks my chair before leaning forward. "Yo, man. That actually makes sense. You're a pretty good wingman."

Sam turns to him again. "Dude. Shut up. This is not your conversation. Go get your own wingman." Sam glances at me and grins. "Thanks for havin' my back."

The good thing about Sam is when he gets irritated, it doesn't last long. He likes being happy too much. Plus, girls make him happy. And everywhere I've been with him, there's always a girl.

Mr. Bell drops his phone on the desk. "What makes a democracy?" he asks. "Anyone?"

"The right to choose," I answer. I like to answer first because that means I get to point out the obvious. The more people answer, the harder it gets to think of something that hasn't already been said.

"That's true, Charlie. You get five points." He scribbles in his notebook. "But I'm looking for more than that." He scans the room. I duck to stare at the words on the page of my textbook. Mr. Bell is like the only teacher I know who insists on using a book instead of a tablet. He says it's out of respect for the original founding fathers who wrote like real men. They dipped their feathers in ink. They contemplated every word they ever wrote because they knew once they wrote it there was no taking it back. Mr. Bell loves everything about the constitution and government and democracy. I do not, which is why I'm glad I have a photographic memory.

The next twenty-seven minutes consist mostly of a class discussion and me taking notes as if I were the class secretary, but I don't mind. Observing and taking notes is one of my favorite things. I think I'm pretty good at it. I look up at the clock. The school day is almost over. I'm more than ready to go home. It's been an exceptionally long day.

"So I hear there's a new girl and she's named after a planet," some guy whispers in the back row.

"Is she hot?" someone else asks.

My stomach hurts. I think I need to go back to the nurse's office. I look up at the clock. There's six and-a-half minutes until the bell rings. I wonder if I could hang out in the bathroom that long.

"She's alright," a third person answers. "I'd hook up with her."

My hands tighten along with the rest of me. I want to take the pencil I grip and stab him in the eye so he can't look at Venus. I wish they would shut up. Why isn't Mr. Bell telling them to be quiet? What happened to talking about democracy? "So who shot JFK?" I blurt.

Mr. Bell's head pops up. "Excuse me?"

What am I doing? Why am I shouting? "JFK," I pipe up. "Who shot him?"

"Dude," growls the chair-kicker guy from behind me. "*Shut up.*"

I lean forward and pretend I don't hear him. "Do you really want to know?" Mr. Bell asks.

Not particularly, but I want to hear anything other than the three idiots in the back of the room talking about Venus like she might not be pretty enough to go out with one of them. She's way too good for any of them.

If this were the ocean and I were a Killer whale *I'd* make them shut up. Like right now. They're the only mammals that don't have natural predators. Killer whales rule the ocean. But I'm just me, and this is high school. I'm pretty much nonexistent unless academics are involved and the teacher leaves the room because he can't hold his coffee. Then everyone acts like I'm as cool as being Sam Birk's best friend, which sounds stupid. Because I *am* his best friend. Except when he's not around. Then I'm pretty much invisible unless test grades are at stake. On test day, they swarm me like a little lost school of fish to look over my shoulder at my answers.

Mr. Bell taps his sneaker-covered toe. Their not-so-quiet whispers flood my ears. They're still talking about her. They leave me no choice. "Yes. I'd like to know your theories on the shooting of America's greatest President," I answer Mr. Bell.

Our teacher leans back in his chair with a smile. I rest my elbows on my desk and lean in as far in as is humanly possible. The rest of the class groans. I smile even bigger as Mr. Bell starts talking. If I'm listening to him then I don't have to hear whatever they were going to say next about Venus, the most perfect girl at Seeberger High.

I may not be as intimidating as a Killer whale or as deadly as the Australian box jellyfish, but I know enough about Mr. Bell to silence the back row.

FOUR

Venus

I'm not sure how I feel about Charlie Barren. It feels strange walking around in his room when he's not in it, but Creed insisted it was fine. I glance at my watch for the tenth time. She's been in the bathroom for like sixteen minutes. I feel weird for knowing it to the minute, but she walked in there at 3:47 p.m., and she said Charlie would be home any time, and that me walking around his room would give me a better idea of what sort of project to do with him for Spanish class. Other than discovering she wasn't kidding about his fixation with becoming a marine biologist, I'm not sure what I'm supposed to find here that will help me with coming up with an idea for Spanish class.

Books on plants and animals line the bookshelves. The bookshelves are as tall as me and cover every inch of the wall. He has more shelves hanging here and there. They're covered with glass figurines of fish. His headboard has all different sorts of rubber fish lying in all different ways. His comforter is one big ocean wave. I plop down on the corner of his bed and pull up the picture on my phone of the assignment checklist once more. I wait for inspiration to hit before I fall back on my back to stare at his ceiling.

"You're in my bed," he remarks.

I lift my chin and dig the top of my head deeper into the comforter as I look at him from upside down. "Yes I am."

"Why?"

"I was thinking," I begin.

"About what?"

"Ideas for our Spanish project," I answer.

"And did you think of one?"

I close my eyes and slowly relax my neck. "No," I answer as I cross my arms. "Did you?"

I'm not watching him anymore. It makes my head and neck hurt. Rolling my eyes in the back of my head to look up and backward at the same time feels unnatural. "We could watch a Spanish soap opera and dissect the dialogue," he offers.

I giggle. "That's not a bad idea, except what sort of contribution are we making to humanity if we watch some of the worst excuse for acting and then force it upon our peers?"

He chuckles. It's kind of cute. "You're painfully truthful," he whines to me, but it feels like a compliment.

"I guess so."

"I like you." He clears his throat. "I mean, I like that about you."

I don't know what to say. "Either is fine."

He blinks. I think my words just caught up to him. His face is pink. It's utterly adorable. He tosses a hand on his hip. "So. What are we doing then?"

I shrug. "No se. Esta su escuela."

"No, no, no. Escuela esta por tu. Tambien. Tu es muy inteligente. Como, dice, 'si se puede,'" he prompts.

"No quiero," I protest. "We should volunteer in an ESL setting."

"We have teachers for that," he argues.

I shake my head. He's not getting it. "I'm suggesting we go to like the place at the mall or wherever you have one here and we work in a classroom setting with adults learning to speak English. We help them with their resumes. We help them with job searches." I clap my hands. "There is no way we won't get an A if we do this. It involves being peers and it's a public service."

He fidgets. "Did you not hear me say that I am not good with people?" he demands. *But Mom always says change is good, and he is in desperate need of something.*

"There is no time like the present for you to start developing better people skills. You cannot avoid real people all of your life. It doesn't work that way."

He turns just enough to have most of his back to me. "I don't avoid people, Venus. They avoid me." He clears his throat. "And yes, I can avoid people, especially when I become a marine biologist."

I hate myself, but I clap my hands again. This guy needs some serious peppiness. "The time for you hiding in your little shell is over. You're going to go out there and give it your all. If nothing else, it's for your GPA." I give him a tiny shove. "Who knows? You might make a friend or two."

"Or I might be forced to pass out from a crippling anxiety attack that takes me to the floor. If this happens, I blame you," he warns.

I can't help but giggle. "Oh, Charlie, I think I make you swoon," I tease.

He tenses up. All the air leaves the room. Why did I open my big, stupid mouth, and why did a little Southern belle pop out of me? I clear my throat. "So anyway, I'm thinking we could come up with some basic, necessary phrases people use in conversation or like when traveling, and then we teach them those."

He lets out a long sigh from where he stands in the middle of the room. "Fine. But just so you know, I would rather be a mediocre translator in a maximum-security prison or participate in community service while wearing a brightly-colored vest and pick up cans with a fireplace poker than spend the afternoon conversing in Spanglish with illiterate, slightly capable, partially bilingual adults who choose to spend their Saturdays hanging out in the highly visible windowed-room closest to the public bathroom while the rest of the world uses Rosetta Stone or Hooked on Phonics to learn a second language. The art of conversation has been reduced to electronic text messaging, Snapchat, BeReal, and whatever else. This new form of communication has *murdered* our spelling and grammar skills at an appalling rate." He raises his finger. "And I, for one, am okay with that. It matters not to me that the average American's mastering of the English language on the linguistic level is marginal at best."

He opens his mouth to speak once more. I raise my hands in the time-out position that is universally recognized in the sporting world. He closes his mouth.

"Dang, Gilmore girl wannabe, slow your monologue. If you want to hold my hand, just say so. You didn't need to bring the threat of maximum security into it," I joke.

His face turns pinker. "I said nothing of holding your hand. I was merely expressing to you scenarios that would be less unpleasant than assisting perfect strangers in capacities that I am unfamiliar with."

I stand up and give him a playful shove. "No one expects you to be an expert, Charlie. Trust. It'll be a piece of cake. Adults love teenagers taking an interest in anything they do."

He stares at me skeptically.

"For reals," I insist before tilting my head and batting my eyes like a goof. "Would I lie to you?"

He stares at me for the longest time. I think he's actually contemplating my question. "No," he replies. "You wouldn't." Charlie's blind faith in me makes my chest burn and my eyes water. *What is going on*?

"Okay, then," I begin as soon as I find my voice. "Let's head to the mall. Shall we?"

His pink cheeks pale. "Right now?"

I nod. "Si. Ahora. Mrs. Hernandez said we're already two weeks behind. There's no time like the present to get started."

"Okay. We will go to the mall right now," he whispers like he's in a trance. We gaze into each other's eyes for forever. It's so awkward, but I can't stop. Charlie looks away first. He marches out of the room. I follow.

For half a second, I forget who I'm with until it hits me between the eyes as we're walking out the front door. I snap my fingers. "Hold up. Where's Creed?"

He pivots. I'm mid-step. My forehead sort of bounces off his chin. I should back away. I don't. He should move somewhere besides standing in front of me with his chin almost touching my forehead. He doesn't. I stare at a second tiny mole on the side of his neck. It's just the right size and shape. I must be crazy. "Where is she?"

"The bathroom." The special moment is gone. There's no way to say *bathroom* and sound sexy even though I'm so close to him I think I smell his neck.

"Right," he says as he scoots past me while I lean/faint into the doorframe. *What the heck am I doing? I can't fall for the nerd, no matter how hot his blushes are.*

Creed's the first friend I've made at the new school, and she's great. I doubt she'll be too excited about me falling her big brother. I turn and glance at the pictures lining the walls. There are photos of a dark-headed, sober boy who looks a little lost. I step closer, and that's when I see it. He's turned away from the camera. He's pointing at something. Half his face is what the camera caught, but that half is illuminated,, and it's not just the fireworks in the night sky. He's filled with so much joy and excitement that he can't be captured by a single photo. The rest of the picture is dark. I wonder what he saw.

"Creed," he yells from somewhere else in the house. "We're going to the mall. Spanish assignment. We'll be back later."

My phone vibrates in my pocket.

CREED:

R u fr going 2 the mall w/my bro?

VENUS:

Spanish project. We r partners. I need this grade.

CREED:

Got it.

34

VENUS:

U want me to wait 4 u?

CREED:

Nah. Killer stomachache.

VENUS:

So sorry. Can I get u anything?

CREED:

Nah. Next time don't let me eat so much.

VENUS:

K? Of what?

CREED:

Everything. LOL.

VENUS:

I will try. TTYL.

CREED:

Yep.

"What are you looking at?" he asks.

I glance up from Creed's last message. "Nothing. Just checking in with your sister." I point to the photo of him. "What were *you* looking at?" I tease in what I hope is a flirty voice, but at the same time I don't. I really want to know.

His face breaks out in a smile; one I haven't seen yet. One that makes me want to ask the same question ten more times. "It was the fourth of July," he muses as he saunters over.

"You a big fireworks fan," I tease again.

His shy guy face is back, and I am in serious like. His sneaky smile that suggests pure joy mixed with a little mystery remains. "They're alright, but that wasn't it. It was the first time I'd been to the ocean."

The longing in his voice is palpable. "You really love the water," I remark.

He nods. "I do." He fiddles with an invisible string at the bottom of his shirt. "So much so that I threw the one and only fit I ever have thrown when we left to go back home."

I can't help but giggle. "I can't imagine you doing that."

His eyes sparkle and shine upon me. "Well, I did. Screamed and cried like the baby I was being, and when that didn't work I refused to eat. For two whole days. I wouldn't speak to anyone. I hardly used the bathroom." He fidgets. "My mother was ready to take me to the emergency room."

My eyes widen. "Seriously?"

He turns to the photo. "Yeah."

"What about your dad?"

He makes a funny sound and smirks. "The last place he was going to take me was the hospital. After three days of being on the road, and my mom shedding a few tears, he took me inside the boy's bathroom. He warned me that if I didn't stop acting like a little turd, that was the last time he took me to any ocean."

I stare at the little boy in the picture once more. "And did it work?"

He picks up the photo, running his finger over it. "Yeah. I can be stubborn when I want my way, but so can my dad. I knew his threat wasn't just a threat. He meant it."

The dreamy look on his face tears me in two. I know he's not thinking about me. "So the ocean put that big of a smile on your face?"

He holds the picture closer, as if he's trying to see something that's not there. "Not just the water. I saw a killer whale. It jumped up out of the ocean and went back into the waves." His awe gives me the shivers, but his eyes almost plead. "I really did."

"And no one else saw," I add.

He sets the picture down. "No. They didn't."

"And I'm gonna guess they didn't believe you."

He gives me a small grin. It's kind of sad. "Just like you don't."

I lay my hand on his about the time I realize it's a weird thing to do. I take it back and walk toward the front door. I need some space. "I believe you," I call as I step outside and pull out my phone for something to look at besides him, but it's kind of hard. I'm standing outside a locked car, and he holds the key. So why isn't he unlocking it?

"Are we going or what?" I ask.

He just keeps staring. "Why did you touch my hand?"

I want to be anywhere but here. I made a perfectly normal moment awkward by touching his hand, but now he's making it mega weird. And now I'm kind of mad at him. Why did he have to say it out loud? "It felt right, but now it doesn't," I tell him. "Don't make it weird." My voice sounds harsher than I wanted, but this is so embarrassing.

He hits the key fob before dropping the keys on the ground. I pull on the door handle. It opens. Thank God. I climb inside.

A second later his door opens. He sits behind the wheel, sticks the key in the ignition, and turns it. "So we're going to the mall."

I nod. "Yes." I feel him staring at the side of my face as I look down at my phone. I don't know why I'm googling directions. I'm sure he knows how to get there. This town isn't that big. It's not like I'm going to get lost. "What?" Why isn't he backing up?

"I didn't mind your hand. It was nice."

I stare straight ahead. I'm two seconds from getting out of the car. "That's great. Can we just go?"

He checks his mirrors like ten times before inching out of the driveway as slow as a vision-impaired turtle that's like 200 years old. The car is too quiet. I want to reach out and turn on his radio, but that would be rude. I think. But him not asking me what music I want to listen to is rude. I think. I don't know.

I've only had one other boyfriend. His name was Josh. He was so cute. And he was funny. But sometimes, he was too much. Like he loved to prank, but sometimes he forgot to stop. Thinking about him makes me smile, though. I can't help it. He would not like Charlie. He would probably call him Charles.

"What are you smiling about?" Charlie asks as he drives exactly two miles under the speed limit.

"My boyfriend," I answer. "I mean my ex-boyfriend." I stare

out the window. I'm still not ready to look at Charlie after what he said to me about my hand and his hand.

"Oh," he mumbles. Now I feel bad.

"He was a joker, and he made me smile," I explain.

"You liked to be tricked?" Charlie cries. That is a normal response, but he's so literal. He doesn't get it.

"No. I don't like to be tricked," I protest while I stare harder out the window. "You know what, just forget it." I swear. I can't even have a normal conversation with this guy. Whatever made me think we might be good together? A relationship can't start because of one adorable picture of half a kid's face. I shove my hands between my mid-thighs. Besides, a whale made him over-joyed. I can't compete with an entire ocean.

"Then what do you mean?" Charlie insists. He sounds so honest. I guess I'm not used to someone wanting a real answer. He's probably not going to like what I have to say.

"Like when we were in the car, he would ask me what kind of music I like," I begin, but then I stop. I feel so stupid. Charlie's not going to get it.

"And then what?"

"And then I would pick a song on the radio, and then he would either start singing all the wrong words to it really loud, or he would turn the station repeatedly," I continue.

"Why would he do that?"

I tap my toes on the floorboards. I knew he wouldn't get it. "Because that's just his way. He liked to be goofy."

"Sounds kind of annoying to me," Charlie snorts. And I agree. That's one of the reasons we broke up. That and I caught Josh talking to another girl about a month before I moved. It was all so dumb. I was the one who told him we should break up because it wouldn't work, because long distance never does. He was the one who insisted it would work. He got all sappy and swore he'd write me letters and drive the six hours on the week-ends just to see me even though he had sports commitments, which I reminded him of. My eyes water. I'm being ridiculous. Josh and I broke up like three months ago. We were together eight months though. That's kind of a long time. He was my first ever boyfriend.

"Well, he wasn't," I whisper. "He was funny."

He taps his thumb on the steering wheel. "If you say so." He pulls into the parking lot. "Did you love him?"

I flinch at his question. Why do boys always want to know that? Like every show I've ever watched, that's the first thing they ask when they hear the girl had a boyfriend before them. There's never a right answer. If you don't love the guy you were with, you're like a cold-hearted witch. If you say you loved him, then the next guy is always thinking you're thinking about the first guy. "I'm fifteen," I answer.

He just keeps staring. It's kind of weird. "I'm eighteen," he replies.

I put my hand on the door handle. "Well good for you. Maybe you'll get drafted."

Half a second passes. I don't know why I said what I just said. It had nothing to do with what we were just talking about. He probably thinks I'm some sort of socially-challenged weirdo. Laughter pours out of him. He leans back in his seat and guffaws. I'm all warm inside. "You're hilarious," he gets out between more howling.

I feel so smart, and he's so hot. Especially when he laughs. His eyes are all lit up. He's so happy. I just want to sit here and stare at the side door of the mall with its half-broken sign that has half a bowling ball on it and the tops of two pins and make him laugh more. There are hardly any cars in the parking lot. I wonder if we'll find anyone to help. "Well. You ready to go speak-a some Span-ish?" I ask in my best fake Spanish-American accent. "Andale."

"Do you always go around looking for random strangers who don't speak English to help?" he asks over the front of the Forester, but I don't think he's teasing. He's too serious for that.

"Maybe." I continue staring ahead. "What's the name of the mall?"

"Seriously." He steps closer to me. "There's only one shopping mall in this town, and we're already here. Why do you need the name? We're not a metropolis."

"For this not being a metropolis, it sounds to me like you have diversity."

He rolls his eyes. He might be Creed's brother after all. "Puh-lease. We have diversity because we have two plants in town and a couple of orchards. We have the type of environment that offers jobs that Caucasian men are allergic to, and so others fill those jobs." He stands with one hand on the door handle. "However, the irony is that the same men who do not want to work those jobs that help sustain our economy that struggles more and more each day are the ones who don't want minorities here."

I scan the place. No one is listening. I lean in. "Sounds about right. They won't want immigrants coming in, but they don't want to work the jobs the immigrants fill, the same jobs that help keep this nation afloat and feed them fresh fruit and veggies they can afford."

He nods. "Yep. Just like they don't support outsourcing, but they also wouldn't want to have to buy the same products for a lot more money if the United States did not outsource. Can you imagine the cost of an Apple product if China didn't make them?"

My stomach hurts at the thought of not having my phone. It's just sad. "No. I can't. I'm embarrassed to admit I don't know where I'd be without my iPhone, iPad, and laptop. It's bad."

He taps my phone screen with his finger. "You know they built a fence—"

"Around the factory where they make Apple products, so the overworked, exhausted workers cannot jump off the top of the building and commit suicide? Yeah. I knew that. But heaven help us if we stop selling iPhones or make the product in such a way it's so expensive half the country can't buy one."

He nods again as he opens the door to the mall. "Exactly."

I can't help but smile. I can't believe how much we agree on.

"Shall we go in?" he asks.

I step inside.

FIVE

Charlie

I can't believe how much I've spoken to a fifteen-year-old girl who is my sister's best friend, just like I can't believe I'm following her into my perfect nightmare: speaking to complete strangers in a language I have not mastered with a girl that I might like. An inevitable epic failure. Venus might just be the living embodiment of the Venus flytrap. Dionaea muscipula. She's drawing me in. I'm like a helpless fly who cannot stay away from her beauty. She's going to rip my heart out and eat me alive. And I will enjoy every twisted minute of it. I had no idea being a social martyr could be captivating and terrifying all at the same time.

"Charlie?" Venus holds the door open. It's my last chance for escape. Why can't I be like all the jocks who hang out at the sports store pretending to check out shoes, when they're really waiting for hot girls to come in and peruse the sports bra racks while pretending they're not ogling said hot guys? All this pretending is so exhausting.

I would know. My sister Creed is an expert at the art of pretending to shop for clothes when she's *really* shopping for her next romantic Snapchat victim to start an online relationship with. She'd agonize for days over meeting him in person to go on a date, and then promptly stop talking to him once they meet up and she discovers his hamartia. Then she'd agonize for the next week over their eventual breakup, depending on if they can coordinate their bus schedules. Creed has done this at least five times. I don't know how she's still sane. It's emotionally draining for me, and all I am is her unwilling viewer.

I walk past Venus to step into her lair. I am not Creed. I don't have the strength and endurance to feign shopping for a pair of shoes. I'm the introverted guy prepared to suffer many moments of awkward silence and embarrassment for a good grade in a class I had no intentions of taking until the perfect girl showed up and disrupted what was supposed to be my last boring year of high school. And I was fine with spending my last year of high school with my nose in the books.. What I'm not fine with is the fact that another homo sapiens exists who I want to ignore but cannot ignore but she seems fine with ignoring me at the moment. Mostly. She motions at me behind her back with one finger. I think she wants me to come talk to the lady she's talking to. But she's not using her friendly finger.

I approach with caution. "My name is Venus, and this is Charlie. We attend Seeberger High School. We are in Mrs. Hernandez's classroom. I saw online that you offer times for English-speaking persons to spend time with Spanish-speaking persons and so I thought that would be something that we could do." She leans in a little. "We also have an assignment in Spanish class, and I thought this would be a good fit for that."

The lady taps her fingertips on the table. "Well, now. I don't know if we have any regulars per se right now. It's been a little while."

Venus's shoulders droop. Her face falls. I'm not that great at reading emotion, but even I can tell she's disappointed. "Okay, well. Can I like leave my cell number with you in case something pops up?" she hesitates. "Marti."

I note Marti's name on the nametag she's wearing. Venus makes this all look so easy. My stomach churns so hard it's a wonder I don't poop out butter. I'm so glad she didn't make me talk to the lady behind the table. I wish I could think of something to say to give Venus some hope. I didn't think it was the best idea, but now that it's not working and she's so sad about it, I feel kind of bad. "Is there anything else we can do to interact with Spanish-speaking people?" I blurt.

Marti's eyes widen. Venus gives me a dirty look before turning back to Marti. "He didn't mean it like that, mam. He's just very serious about his grades."

Yes, I did mean it like that. I meant exactly what I said. Otherwise, I would not have said it. What's so bad about being honest?
Marti runs her fingers along the side of the table. "Well. There is a quinceañera going on today at the community building. It's in about an hour. I suppose you could go in my place." She fidgets. "I was invited but I couldn't go because I'm working. I didn't really want to go anyway." She looks off to the side. "Big parties and loud music make me nervous. I'm not a very good dancer. I don't like eating strange foods." She ducks behind the table before coming back up with her purse. She digs through it. "Now where is that invite?" she mutters just as a red corner covered in gold glitter pokes out of her purse.

Venus grabs it as if it were always hers. I have the urge to pinch myself. I can't believe this is happening. "Here," she chirps. "I found it."

The lady frowns, but I don't know why. That's what she said she was looking for. "Well, I'm not entirely sure if you should go. You don't really know her."

Venus takes me by the hand. I had negative thoughts about crashing the party, but they're gone now. I can't think past her hand in mine and how badly I want it to stay there. "Thanks," she tells the woman behind the table as she yanks me across the room. "We'll put your name on the card."

Venus jogs down the middle of the mall. Her hand is still in mine. That must be why I'm running through the mall like a maniac. She lets go. I can't believe how lost I feel.

"There," she proclaims. "There's a bath bomb store. It's perfect."

We jog through the kid's play area in the middle of the mall to get to the bath bombs. Venus has a black mesh bag on her arm and two things already in it by the time I get to her. "You don't know if she likes this stuff," I argue.

She makes crazy eyes at me. I love it. "Um, hel-lo? What teenage girl doesn't love pretty smelling stuff that glitters as it disintegrates and transforms into foam bubbles? Chemistry doesn't get better than that," Venus teases. If I wasn't in love with her before, I am now. Her rationality annihilates whatever words of protest I was about to utter next. She doesn't even know. She's too busy studying the Clearance section with the fixed focus of a specialist disabling an explosive device. If she's anything like my sister, we're going to be here all day. I can't believe I'm thinking of my sister when I'm standing next to Venus, who draws me in like a lantern fish. If she's got shark teeth behind all her blinding light, I don't care. She can rip me to shreds. It would be a beautiful death.

Her searching eyes fly to her watch. "Crap balls. We have forty-two minutes until the party starts."

"The party we're going to crash," I add, because I want to be sure we're still doing this, but also because it sounds kind of cool. And I have never been cool.

She steps up on me and gets in my space. I hate people getting in my bubble. But not her. She can stay here indefinitely. In fact, I could make allowances and have a two-person bubble.

"Yes, Charlie. The party we're going to crash," she whispers, staring up at me like I'm a genius. I so want to be.

"Okay," I reply. She returns to contemplating how much money to spend on a complete stranger. This goes on for the next six minutes. I'm a clock watcher. I can't help it. The second hand's steady pattern soothes me.

"Charlie. Get over here," she commands.

I rush to her side. "What?"

She looks inside her shopping bag which now holds five items. "How much money needs to be spent to be forgiven for crashing someone's party?" she muses.

I consider her question. I have no idea. "How much would *you* need?" I ask. My therapist once told me that if I am ever in doubt in how to respond appropriately, it is always best to reflect the person's question back on them.

She snaps her fingers. "You're freaking brilliant." She puts two items back and winks at me. "Here's to hoping she's as cheap as I am," she chirps before marching toward the cashier. Seconds later, we walk out. "Now. We need to go to a dollar store to buy chocolate and a pretty bag to put this all in."

"But what if she doesn't like—"

Her finger is glued to my lips. I don't know why. I don't care. A girl has never touched my lips before. Especially not one that I find remotely interesting. And Venus is way more than remotely interesting.

"*Shut up, Charlie.* You know *nothing* about girls. We really are pretty simple creatures. We like nice-smelling things and chocolate. And this definitely calls for a chocolate emergency."

I resist the urge to bite her finger. Or kiss it. My feelings scare me. I don't know what to do. Why won't she move it away from my face? I back away from her. "Fine. I'll take you to the dollar store. Just stop touching me," I growl. I don't understand myself. Why did I tell her to stop when all I want is for her to do it more?

She stops moving. "If you don't want to go with me to the party, just say so," she huffs.

"I never said I didn't want to go." I hit the unlock button.

She climbs in the car. So I do the same. She stares straight ahead. So I do the same. I don't know what else to do. "You could always take me to the dollar store and drop me off at the party. I can find my own ride home. I've done it before."

The thought of her riding home with another guy fills me with uncertainty. I do not like this feeling. I clench my fists. What is going on with me? Where are all these emotions coming from, and why do they change so quickly? "That's not a good idea," I manage.

She laughs at me.

"What's so funny?" I demand.

"That's not a good idea," she mimics before turning to at me. "You're not my dad."

I'm so confused. "I never said I was your dad. I'm just saying, don't you ever watch true crime shows?" I don't, but Creed does, and then she like relays the whole story line to me. Every time. Even though I've told her I don't want to know. Multiple times. She just keeps going. I've found it's easier to listen for five minutes instead of arguing for fifteen minutes about why I don't want to hear it. In the end, I'll listen to it because Creed is very persistent.

"No. I don't watch true crime shows. They're annoying. I know how to be aware. I also carry mace. If you don't want to go with me, I'm sure Creed will." She smiles in a different way. I don't think I like it. "Maybe Creed and I will meet a couple of hotties, and they can teach us how to *polka*."

"Polka music is for grandpas. Have fun with that," I snort as I drive a few blocks to the dollar store.

"For your information, polka music is not just for grandpas," she hollers. Why is she so mad? "It's their culture. And since this party is for a fifteen-year-old girl, I'm sure there will be plenty of teenage boys there for me to dance with." She hops out. I jog to catch up to her. She's screaming at me in the middle of the parking lot. People are staring.

I'm out of breath. She's a power walker. She flings the door open to the dollar store. It almost hits me in the face. "Can you keep your voice down, please?" I whisper. She jerks away.

"Why? Do you not want others to hear you're concerned a *stranger* might try to *kidnap me*?" she yells.

This is so weird. Why is she acting like this? What did I do to make her so upset? "I was before, but now I'm not." I answer. Because it's the truth. If she's this loud in public, I seriously doubt anyone will try to take her anywhere against her will.

A lady down the aisle from us giggles. I could be wrong, but I think she's laughing at Venus, who yanks a colorful paper bag off the hook and slaps it against my chest. "Hold this," she demands. I cover it with my hand just as she bends over to pick up some other type of colorful paper. "Stick that in the bag," she orders.

"Okay," I reply, even though I want to walk back outside. If she were Creed, I would. I don't put up with people being rude to me. But she's not Creed. She's kind of sort of still the girl of my dreams. I think. At least she was until she started yelling at me in the middle of the parking lot and then in the store about being kidnapped. I follow her to the candy aisle. She grabs a box of hot tamales, a box of sour gummy worms, and a bag of chocolate.

I wrinkle my nose. "You really eat all that together?"

She rolls her eyes. "A girl likes to have choices." She glances at her watch again. "Ugh. Now we only have twenty-seven minutes. I have no idea what I'm going to wear."

We walk to the front of the store. I stand beside her at the checkout lane. "That'll be fourteen dollars and thirty-six cents," the lady says. I wait for Venus to pay. She doesn't. She's too busy staring at her phone. A line forms behind us.

"Are you going to pay?" I ask her. The woman at the register gives me a dirty look. "This isn't my idea," I tell the lady behind us, who continues to stare.

Venus looks up. "This is *your* grade too."

I dig the twenty from my pocket, the one I've been saving since three weeks ago. I hardly ever spend money, but I like to have it on me in case I find something I absolutely must have. That does not include candy for a girl I've never met. Even if we are crashing her party. I better get an A in Spanish III.

The lady at the register slaps my change into my hand kind of hard. Venus already has it all bagged up. She's halfway to the door. "Hurry it up already, cheapskate. You're holding up the line," the woman with three kids hanging off her snaps before I rush after Venus. I guess I don't need a receipt, but I feel incomplete.

We get back in the Forester. "So I can go home now," I begin.

Venus snaps her seatbelt in place. "Yeah." She stares at me. "Is that what you're wearing to the party?"

I lay a hand on my sweatshirt, the one my grandma got me from one of her first road trips after she retired. It's soft, fuzzy, and faded. It's my favorite because it has a Killer whale on it. "What do you want me to wear?"

She shrugs. "Do you have any button-up shirts? How about a pair of boots?"

My brain hurts. She's asking too many questions about things I do not care a whit for. "I don't wear that. I live in Moscow," I joke. "We are all communists. Personal expression is not allowed."

She gives me a playful shove. "You live in Idaho."

I shrug. "I know where I live. I prefer comfort. I do not enjoy wearing things that squeeze my toes or pinch my fingers."

She giggles. It's adorable. "Pinch your fingers?"

I look over at her. "You ever try to button up a guy's shirt? The buttons are super tiny. I like anything I can pull over my head."

She stares at my hair. "But then you'll mess up all that beautiful hair," she teases.

I blush. Mom says I got the best hair in the family. I feel bad that I'm probably a little too proud of it. "It's just hair," I reply. I don't know what else to say. Somehow, we're in my driveway. I don't remember getting here.

She jumps out of the car, the one I'm not supposed to be driving because I don't have a license. What is it about this girl that makes me totally lose my head? The front door to the house flies open, interrupting my miniature panic attack about accidentally breaking the law because being around Venus makes me temporarily insane. "We're gonna crash a party," Creed hollers. "This is so epic! You are the bomb!" She points at someone or something, I'm not sure. "You drive a Forrester! We drive a Forrester! Twinning is winning!"

They side hug each other while Creed Snaps a thousand pictures with her phone in the span of five seconds. I start up the steps to the house. "Does he have to come?" Creed whines.

"Yes. He's our ride," Venus responds. "Unless he changes his mind." I walk past them.

"I'm not changing my mind," I retort. "This is our project. Mrs. Hernandez said."

SIX

Venus

I follow Creed up to her room. She throws her door open. There are piles and piles of clothes on her bed. I can't believe I was worried about finding something to wear. "I wanted to give you lots of options," she proclaims. It sounds like an apology. I don't know why.

"Gi-rl. You're so awesome. This is going to be so great," I tell her.

She giggles and claps her hands. "No. You're awesome. I've never crashed a party. Like, *never*. I thought I would like have to wait until college, or at least until I'm out of this place. It's so boring. Nothing ever happens here."

I snatch up a glittery sweater and dance around the room. "It's not boring anymore," I sing. Today is going to be so much fun." I look over at her. "But I have to like make some TikToks or something at the party. You know, to prove I'm like having conversations and stuff. For Spanish class. For my grade."

She nods. "Definitely." She waves her finger. "But also, we're going to totally find some cute guys to dance with."

I glance at my watch again. "We gotta hurry. We only have like nineteen minutes."

She makes bug eyes at me. "You do realize they're Hispanic,

right? Like the joke of their culture being on their own time? It's not a joke."

I pause for half a second. "Yeah, but this is a quinceañera. I don't want to be rude."

She raises an eyebrow. "Even though we're crashing their party?"

I giggle. I can't help it. I'm so excited. "But we're bringing her a present, and we're going for Marti."

She stands in front of the mirror, moving around in her oversized, off-the-shoulder velvet top. It's killer on her. "Who's Marti?"

"The lady they know at the mall," I answer.

"That's so smart," she exclaims.

"I know." As if I'm like super smart and not some desperate teenage girl determined to prove to Charlie, Mr. Negativity, that my idea for getting a good Spanish grade will work. And maybe a small part of me wants to impress him. So what if he's eighteen and I'm fifteen? That doesn't mean he knows everything. That doesn't mean I'm useless. I've been coming up with all the ideas today. Mostly.

"So do you think your brother will change his outfit?" I ask.

Creed laughs. "It's not likely, but that doesn't matter. No one notices Charlie. He's happy being a wallflower and most people are happy that he is." She applies her lip gloss.

"That was kind of mean," I remark.

She puts the lid back on before leaning in to start on her mascara. "It's not mean, Venus. Trust me. The last thing my brother wants to be is the life of the party. He is a mega introvert. It's just who he is."

Hearing her talk about her brother like that saddens me. I must have made him super nervous all day today, but he didn't act it. He could have stayed in the car when we went to the mall but he didn't. He could have kept his mouth shut when I talked to Marti, but he didn't. He didn't have to follow me into the dollar store, and he doesn't have to go to this party. I glance in the mirror once more. I don't usually wear white jeans, royal blue sweaters with scattered green leaves on them, and taupe-colored boots. I like dark jeans, pink sweaters, and tennis shoes. But Creed has excellent taste in fashion, and she said the bits of green in the sweater brings out my eyes, along with the killer wingtips and eye shadow she put on me in about three seconds. She's a hair and makeup magician. The high ponytail and tight braid doesn't feel like me either, but she said we are being respectful of their culture. I knock on Charlie's door.

"What?"

I turn the knob. He stands in the middle of the room in a half-buttoned-up shirt and black slacks. I walk over. His fingers fumble with the buttons. He wasn't joking. He looks like he's in physical pain. I swat his hands away. "Here. Let me," I say as I stare at the ribbed white tank he wears underneath his plaid green and grey shirt. "You look nice," I offer as I work on his buttons.

"Thanks," he says. "You look..." he stops talking. I look up at him. "Shiny," he finishes. I have the sudden urge to wipe the lip gloss from my lips that feel all sticky and weird.

"Thanks. Creed helped me."

"That sounds about right." he chortles.

I stop at the last button. "I think that's good enough. You don't want to feel like you're choking."

He turns to the mirror. "I don't have a cowboy hat."

I scoot closer. We've only just met. I don't know how I know, but I do. Neither of us looks like who we are, but together we look just right. I give him a conspiratory wink in the mirror. "Shall we go crash this party, imposter?"

He takes my hand in his, startling us both. "Like a piñata," he replies, giving my hand a squeeze.

Suddenly, I hear footsteps. I let go of his hand and step away.

Creed pops in. "I thought you were in the bathroom."

"I was making sure our driver is ready," I reply.

She rolls her eyes. "C'mon then. Let's go."

I follow her downstairs. A loud shaking sound behind me makes me turn. Charlie stands at the top of the steps. "You forgot something."

I run back up to grab the party gift for the birthday girl. "Thanks."

Twenty-two minutes and three wrong turns later, we arrive at the address on the card. There are two cars in the parking lot. Creed is out of the Forester first. I slowly open my door. Charlie sits in the back seat.

"What are you waiting for?"

"An invitation. This is a bad idea," he mumbles.

I ignore the sinking feeling in my stomach. I don't know this girl, but I wouldn't mind a stranger coming to my party if they brought me something, right? I scan the parking lot. The idea that no one is coming to her party makes me very sad.

"Charlie. Get your ass out of the car," I order before slamming the door a tiny bit for good measure. I stare through the window at him.

I dangle the car keys. He moves in slow motion to open his door before crawling out of his seat like an old man. He grabs the keys from my hand. "Just in case I want to hang out here." Then he locks the car multiple times. It keeps honking.

"Stop it, Charlie," Creed orders.

He shoves the keys in his pocket. We walk up to the door decorated by one sad, sinking, pink balloon. Creed yanks it open. We step inside a long hallway. We move in the direction of the music. A girl in a princess dress wearing a sparkly tiara sits behind an empty table that holds a big, beautiful cake. She looks as if she's about to cry. A couple stands in the next room. I think they're her parents. "Marti sent us," Creed calls.

The girl manages a small smile. "Gracias. Conoces Marti?" she asks the empty room.

"Si," a deep voice answers. We all turn to see who is talking. I can't help it. He sounds like Marco off *The Kissing Booth* movie. If his face is half as sexy as his voice, Creed and I just found our dancing partner. A guy steps out from behind the half wall that bears a Men's Restroom sign on it. He wears a black hoodie, faded blue jeans, and Air Jordans. I think I catch a dirty look from Charlie. I feel silly for making him wear plaid.

"Habla ingles," Creed begins.

"Si," the boy in the hoodie answers before strutting over to Creed and I as we stand in the middle of the room. His hand is out. "Hola. Me llamo Santhiago, but you can call me Santi." His thumb skates over the back of my hand even though he's giving Creed a serious once-over. Whoa. He is smooth.

"Santi," his mother scolds. "Vamanos aqui. Ahora." There's alarm in her voice. What's that about?

I follow Creed over to the table. She holds out the gift bag. "Here. Feliz cumpleaños."

"Thank you," the girl answers. Her lip trembles. "I don't mean to be ungrateful. It's just that we were expecting mi familia, but a bunch of them got sick, and then there was a funeral, but my parents already reserved this for today, and we can't move the date. And they paid for the cake. Now, nobody will eat it. No one is coming to my party."

I hardly know this girl, but this is awful. "Do you have food here?" I ask.

She nods. "And do you have music?" I add.

She shakes her head. "No. Mi hermano Santi was supposed to have connections with his friends two states away. They have a band, but their van broke down and they can't get here."

Creed leans in. "How old is your brother?"

The girl giggles. "He's twenty-one, so watch out. He's sort of girl crazy, but he treats girls like they're women, if you know what I mean."

I throw up a little in my mouth. The guy is hot, but he's not worth breaking the law. "Thanks for the warning," I reply. "Your cake is gorgeous, and so is your dress."

She glances down at her hands in her lap. "Thank you." Her lips tremble again. "My parents did all this for me, and now no one will see it."

I squeeze her hand. "Hey. Just give me and Creed a second or two. We'll come up with a plan. You don't mind if other people our age come to your party, do you?"

She glances up at me again. "You can do that?"

"I think so."

Creed clears her throat beside me. "You can?"

I keep myself from glaring back at her. Barely. "We're going to try." Then I walk back over to Charlie.

"Well, this is a bust. Can we go now?" His whining and readiness to give up so easily are not attractive.

I step closer before I squeeze his lower arm.

"Ouch," he cries.

"Shut up," I snarl. He tries to move away, but I keep a hold as I look up at him. I wish I had a chair to stand on. I feel less threatening when I have to look up at the guy I'm bossing around. "Creed and I are going to help this girl have a party because her parents paid to rent this building and they got delicious food and a beautiful cake. If you don't want to be a part of helping her have the terrific fifteenth birthday that she deserves, then you can leave." I'm totally talking out my butt, as my ex-boyfriend Josh used to love to say, but I don't care. This is for a good cause.

"How are you going to do that?"

"By sending out a school-wide email. Do either of you know how to do that?"

He frowns. "No."

Their answer frustrates me, but I'm not ready to give up. "Do either of you know anyone who knows a lot of people?"

"No." He's determined to rain on my parade.

"What about Sam?" I ask out of desperation. I hardly know him, but he's Charlie's best friend, and he's definitely popular.

Creed shakes her head vigorously. "No. He would never..." she stops talking as she looks over at the sad birthday girl. "I'm just saying this isn't like his scene, or whatever. He would so not invite people here."

At least she has the good sense to whisper.

An idea pops into my brain. It's not the best one, but it's the only one I've got. "What about a public library? Do you have one of those? And what about like gaming or anime groups? Do you have any of those?"

Charlie and Creed look at me like I'm crazy. Maybe I am. I

don't know. But people are coming to this party one way or another. I get on my phone and search. While I'm doing that, I glance at the two of them. "You know what? You can give up or you can try, and I'm not ready to give up, so..."

I don't know what's gotten into me, other than the words of faith Mom always told anyone who would listen to her spouting about the strengths of her one and only daughter/child. "My Venus has more power than people give her credit for. She will not advocate for herself, but by gosh she will advocate for other people. Don't ever tell her what she can or cannot do for someone other than herself, because she will prove you wrong."

"Fine." Charlie sighs while Creed crosses her arms and pouts. I'll make up with her later, or I won't because she'll be thanking me for the crazy amazing crowd that I'm going to get to come here. "What do you want me to say?"

I want to ask him who he's texting, because I seriously doubt any academic club is coming to here either, but he's offering to help, which is more than I can say for his sullen sister. "Just give them the address. The time is NOW. Post free food, cake, and drinks. Epic birthday party. Come as you are to the dance. And post a chance to win fifty dollars," I add.

"I'm not putting up any more money," he argues.

I give him a glare. "I didn't ask you to. *I* have the money. Just post it already." I get on the public library page to type as fast as I can.

"What if no one comes?" Creed whines from across the room. Is she heading for the outside door?

"*This is Idaho.* What else is there to do besides stand around and watch salmon swim upstream?" I pop off.

"We do. We do watch that. It's inspiring," Charlie argues.

"I was being sarcastic," I fire back. It's just him and I. "Where's Creed?" I realize sexy Santi is nowhere to be seen either.

"I'll check the bathrooms," Charlie offers. "She better not be with that guy."

"I agree." I slip out the side door at the back of the room that's propped open by a rock. I spy sexy Santi leaning against the back of his pickup truck. She sits on the end of his flatbed, looking all chill.

"Hey, your brother's looking for you," I warn her.

She swings her legs back and forth. "Yeah, so?"

"If he finds you out here, he's going to make you leave," I tell her. "That would be a pretty crappy thing to do to someone on their birthday." I'm laying it on thick, but I don't care. I can't believe the birthday girl's brother is out here doing nothing when his sister is all alone on her big day.

"We were just talking." Creed hops off the back of his truck and trudges like a turtle over to where I am.

"You gonna swing that swing of yours clean off the back porch?" I grin as she approaches.

"What the heck does that even mean?" She smirks back.

"My mother used to say it. I just said it 'cause it's fun to say," I offer. "Can we please go back inside? Charlie is probably about to have a complete and total meltdown."

We walk back in. Some kind of music I don't recognize is playing, but that's not what holds my attention. Charlie dances in the middle of the room with the birthday girl. Her princess dress floats over the floor. He frowns in concentration as she twirls beneath his hand. My heart melts inside my chest. He shuffles on the cement floor. They come nowhere close to matching the beat of the polka music, but none of that matters. Charlie is the sweetest, sweetest boy. And it is so hot.

"My brother is such a dork," Creed mutters.

"The dorkiest," I reply, but I can't stop smiling. *I so love dorks.*

SEVEN

Charlie

I don't know how I got on the dance floor. All I can say is it probably had a lot to do with a couple arguing very loud and very fast in Spanish, and a very sad girl looking like she wanted to disappear into her chair. That must have been what prompted me to approach her, extend my hand, and ask her to dance.

"Do you want to dance?" I hoped desperately she would say no. I have been turned down as a dancing partner twice. Being rejected as a person and a guy in a public manner is not something I particularly enjoy. The fact that her quarreling parents are the only onlookers helped my self-confidence.

"But there's no music," she replied.

"Do you have music?"

"Yes."

All I know is her parents stopped fighting. So that was good. And she was smiling and not crying. That was also good. I was just following Venus's words that kept going through my head. The ones about trying or not trying. I really hadn't thought about things like that before. Or thought much about anyone else before.

"I am Cristina," the birthday girl began before playing some music on her phone, which she laid back down on the table beside the ginormous cake.

"I'm Charlie," I answered right before she took my hand. I didn't know what to do next so I walked to the middle of the room. "I'm not the best dancer."

She smiled up at me. "It is okay. I know how to dance. Just do what I tell you."

I was so relieved. And so we started dancing. I was so nervous until I decided to pretend I was a fish, and the music was the water, and I should just go with the flow. Things got easier after that. I still have no rhythm, but at least I'm relaxed. Or at least I was relaxed. Until I saw Venus. And now she stands off to the side, looking at me like I'm some sort of hero, which is nice. But I have no idea why. What could my sister possibly have told her between wherever they were before they're back in here?

Santi comes in a different door, which means he was outside. And my sister was outside. That is so not cool. And what about this epic party that my ding-dong sister and her new best friend promised Cristina? So much for that brilliant idea.

"I'm having fun," Cristina says.

I look down at her. I don't like the way she's looking at me like she's waiting for something. It's kind of weird. "I'm glad," I say before going back to looking over at Venus and Creed. Cristina scoots closer, though I don't know how. Her dress is awfully poofy. I drop my elbow so it rests on her collar bone to try to keep space between us.

"Could you move your arm? It's in our way," she huffs.

"Um, sorry. No. I can't. I have like a frozen shoulder," I tell her. I have no idea what I'm saying, but I'm not moving my arm. I danced with her to be nice. She's coming at me like she's a great white shark and I'm some sort of clueless minnow.

"Your arm was fine a second ago," she argues. *What happened to the little sad girl who pouted in the corner? I kind of miss her.*

"It comes on kind of fast," I insist. *Kind of like you.* I'm not about to become her boyfriend. I'm dancing with her to keep her from crying. There's only one girl I might want to date, and it's not Cristina.

Someone jabs me in the back. "Step off, bro. That's my little sister," Santi warns.

I'm so relieved to hear his words, I don't care that he's a little scary. I let go of her waist. "Here. She's all yours," I tell him before bowing. "Thank you for the dance, Cristina."

He gives me a funny look. "What are you doing? This isn't a bull fight. You're not a matador about to die."

"My bad," I mumble before crossing the room to stand by Venus and Creed. "So. What's up? Are we gonna eat or what?"

Venus checks her watch. "Give it a few more minutes. Please. I think people will show up. The message hasn't been out there that long."

As if cued, five teenage boys swagger into the room carrying skateboards. "Yo. We heard there was free food," they crow.

Venus hurries over to them. "There is. There is. Come in the kitchen." She quickly ushers them over to Cristina's parents. Minutes later, the guys have full plates.

"Yo. What about the drawing for the money?" one of the little hoodlums asks.

Venus runs across the room to pluck the biggest sombrero off the wall. She grabs a few sheets of colorful paper and the pair of scissors someone left out. Seconds later, she's handing out paper squares. "Write your name and number on the paper. Fold it in half and drop it in the hat," she says as she points to the upside-down sombrero. "You have to be present to win the cash prize."

"Yo. You never said that," the mouthy one grumps.

She stares him down. "You got somewhere better to be. I don't have the time to track you down. If you want the money, you'll be here." She narrows her eyes at him. "*If* you win."

"Venus is like the perfect party planner. She took over this afternoon like it was nothing. I was ready to give up and go home, but she was so focused on giving Cristina and her parents a day to remember. I never would have thought of any this by myself," Creed chatters away in my ear as we watch from the side.

I turn to her. "What were you doing outside with that guy?"

"Santi? Just chillin'."

"But he's twenty-one."

"Yeah, so?" She nudges me in the ribs with her elbow. "He's hot."

I make the worst face I can think of at her. "You can't make out with him, you know. It's against the law."

"Not if I don't tell." Then she sticks her tongue out at me.

I shove her a little. "That's not funny, and I would so tell."

She glares at me. "Well. You can't make out with Venus. She's fifteen and you're eighteen."

I sweat at the thought of making out. "Three years is better than five," I argue.

"Not when you're sitting in a jail cell," she fires back. Everyone turns to stare at us. I wish I was anywhere but here.

"Good one," I answer just as loudly, but it's a little too late to be anything other than awkward. Cristina gives me an ornery grin before turning up the volume on her phone. She shimmies all the way back to the middle of the floor, but her eyes are on me. I feel hunted and I don't like it. The skaters form some sort of circle around her. They raise their hands and move around. I'm happy to be out of her line of vision.

I'm debating sitting down in the corner or getting some food when someone slips their hand into my elbow.

"Feed me. I'm starving," Venus whines.

"Just stand there looking pretty. Eventually you'll catch something." I may have accidentally made a terrible STI joke.

She pinches the inside of my arm. "I'm going to pretend you're a marine biologist and that was the lamest joke about my name I've ever heard."

I sigh with relief. "It was. Trust me. The words hit me about the time they all came out, and then I wanted to take them back, but they were out there, and..."

She shoves a plate in my hand. "Get me some food and I'll forgive you."

The kitchen counter lined with trays is well hidden from the dance floor. I had no idea there was so much to choose from. I have no idea what she likes. What if I get it wrong? "What do you like?" I ask, but she's halfway across the room, digging in a cooler.

"Just get her tacos," the smiling mom tells me. "Every girl likes tacos."

I hold out the plate. I don't know if I believe her, but I don't know what else to do. "Yes, please."

Seconds later, I have something from every tray on the plate that I only know I'm holding because I feel the bottom of it on the palm of my hand. Otherwise, it would like a bunch of floating food. I didn't know that much stuff could fit on one plate. I go to the nearest table and sit down before I spill it all over the floor.

Venus walks over holding five bottles of pop cradled between her arm and her ribs. "I didn't know which one to choose for you, so I brought them all."

I point at the plate. "Same goes for you."

She giggles. "Well. It looks like we don't need two plates of food. You want to share this plate with me?"

I've never shared food with anyone. Ever. She's asking me to share my germs with her germs. I don't know if I can, but she looks so hopeful. And it would be impolite to say no. "Let me go get two forks," I tell her before making a mad dash to the kitchen.

I can eat off a plate that she's eating from. It's no big deal. If we kiss someday, her saliva will probably end up in my mouth. It's not a big deal, unless she has Hepatitis A or mononucleosis. But she looks pretty healthy. So it's not likely she has either of those things. And she's not homeless or a user of illegal drugs, so that lowers the chances of her getting Hepatitis A by a lot.

I shake my head to clear it. I wish I didn't have such weird, random thoughts. I'm pretty sure no one else in the room is pondering the odds of getting Hepatitis A from eating a plate of food with someone they'd like to date. I grab my fork and two napkins and return to my table.

"Here." She hands me an open bottle of pop.

"You opened it for me. Thanks."

She waves. "Dude. It's not like that. I took a drink. I didn't like it. You can have it."

I stare at the top of the glass bottle as I'm sitting down. There's no way I'm taking a sip of her backwash. There's probably drops of her spit swirling around inside there, coating the sides. I tip the bottle back and forth while looking at the dark brown liquid sloshing back and forth. I think I'm going to be sick. I move the bottle toward my lips. She's watching me. Why is she watching me? Why won't she eat her food? She's probably watching me 'cause I'm acting weird, but I can't help it. I can't do it.

I slam the glass bottle down so hard it shakes the table. "I'm sorry. I don't like root beer."

She raises her brow "That's not root beer. It's Dr. Pepper."

Crap balls. "Well. I don't like that either." I force myself to release the spit-filled bottle before grabbing a capped bottle closest to me. "I'll just drink this."

She wrinkles her nose. "Canada dry? I didn't peg you for a ginger ale kind of guy."

I have no idea what that means. "Well, I am." I cut the end of a pepper looking thing and taking a huge bite. I'll shove anything on my side of the plate in my mouth. I just need to *shut up.*

Someone plops down in the chair across from us. It's Sam. What in the heck is Sam Birk doing at this party?

"Hey, guys. What's up?" He grabs the open bottle I just shoved halfway across the table.

"Venus drank out of that," I reply with my mouth full.

Sam grins at me before giving her a wink. "Her *fineass* lips were on this bottle? Thanks for the heads up." He tips it back and downs half of it. Why can't I be like Sam? He's so cool. He doesn't worry about catching strange viruses because he's too busy focusing on normal things, like how to impress a beautiful girl sitting at a party eating delicious Mexican food. But he doesn't have to try too hard. She's sitting with me, the eccentric germophobe.

I glance over at Venus to see her reaction to Sam joining us. She sips at her pop and watches him, but she doesn't have that look in her eye like so many other girls do when they see Sam. I wish I knew what that means.

She sets her pop bottle down. "This one is *mine*." So don't drink it." She turns back to me. "Thanks for getting me a plate of food, Charlie. It really hit the spot." Her voice is a little softer than it was before. I guess she was really hungry.

"No problem." I take a bite of rice that's near the edge.

"Hold up," Sam barks. "You're eating off her plate." Why does he have to be so loud? And why does he have to notice? He never notices anything that doesn't involve him.

I shrug. "Yeah, so?"

"So you never eat off anyone's plate. Like ever."

What he says is true, but I so wish it wasn't. That should count for something. "I guess I'm hungry."

"And you never eat food that touches other food," he remarks in an accusatory manner.

I grip my fork. What is happening? I never get mad at Sam. He's my best friend. One of my only friends. "I can. I just choose not to."

He glances at Venus and then back at me. His eyes narrow. "No, you can't."

Venus pushes the plate of food at Sam so hard it almost flies off the table, but he catches it, just like it's a football. He's so smooth. "What the hell, girl?"

She stands up. I don't know what to do. I feel like something is going on, but I'm not getting it.

"It sounds to me like you need to carbo load. Your blood sugar must be low or something. That must be why you're talking all crazy to your *best friend*."

Suddenly Creed pops out of nowhere and stands next to Sam. "Hey. It's a birthday party. Everyone needs to chill. Let's drink some pop, eat some food, and dance." She tugs on Sam's arm. "Let's go, Sam. Let's get this party started."

He stares at Venus. She stares right back. "Yeah, Creed. Let's go dance," Sam replies as he gets up out of his chair, throws an arm around her shoulders, and walks toward the dance floor. It's gotten a lot more crowded since I went to the food line. Sam glances back at Venus, who leans across the table to grab her plate of food. She pulls it back in front of us and picks up her fork.

"I'm so glad he didn't touch our food," she tells me. "Then I would have to make you get me another plate." Her hand touches my shoulder. "Watch my stuff? I'll be right back."

I try to watch her plate, but my eyes keep straying to how good she looks in her dark sweater and white jeans. I've never noticed how perfectly a girl's hair can swing back and forth with the rhythm of their step until now. Or maybe no other braid swings as nice as Venus's does. Her braid is mesmerizing, just like her smile as she walks toward me holding a plate in each hand and two more bottles tucked into her side. She sets it all down.

"Here. I got you a little bit of everything, and it's all separated out, just the way you like it."

I feel like I'm five, but I'm also ecstatic. "Thank you."

She forks a bite off her plate, but she doesn't stick it in her mouth. "No one should have to feel uncomfortable or tortured when they're eating," she tells me with a solemn expression. "I'm serious. I don't joke around about food." She nudges me with her elbow she rests on. "Go ahead and enjoy your meal. I know I'm going to." She takes a big bite, closes her eyes, and leans to the side. She side-eyes my uncapped pop. "And I *know* you don't like ginger ale. No one does." She waves her fork at all the other bottles. "Pick another one."

My heart hammers as I study my two plates and the additional capped bottles waiting to be opened. She totally gets me, and she's still here.

$\mathcal{V}$enus

I take a break and sit at the table with Charlie, who is more eccentric than I realized. I'm not sure how I feel about it. "Do you care if I go dance?"

"Not if you don't care that I don't," he answers. "There's too many people." He leans in at the same time I lean in, and our noses touch. His warm breath settles on my lips. It hits me like a freight train. All of a sudden, I'm hot all over. Like *everywhere*. I've never felt this way before, not even when I watch movies with Jacob Elordi, my favorite Hollywood guy crush. There's just something about his character's confidence that gets me, which is hilarious, because in real life if I meet someone that confident, say like Sam Birk, all I want to do is bring them down a notch. They can't help screaming, *Hey, hey, everyone look at me. All the time. I need attention. All the time.*

Charlie's talking to me. I snap out of it. What was he saying? "I'm sorry. What did you say?"

Charlie looks confused. He pulls on my arm until his lips are near my ear. "I said it's super cool you got all these people to come to her party, but I don't like crowded dance floors so I'm just going to stay here."

I nod. I can't think of anything to say when his breath is near my ear. I don't want to like-*like* Charlie. He's graduating soon, and he's totally obsessed with ocean life. But his heart, even though he hides it pretty well, is so big. I can't believe he danced with the birthday girl on an empty dance floor. Or that he forced himself to eat food off my plate when his food issues are something he cannot control. Or that he wore a button-up shirt, something he hates, just for me.

The enormity of his actions makes me like him and dislike him all at the same time. Does love make people crazy? Is that what this is? I can't be in love. I'm only fifteen and we've only just met. I kind of wanted to like a halfway normal guy, but my last boyfriend was like a lot of other guys I know, and he was completely obnoxious. The only reason I didn't dump him sooner is because he was also really hot, he dressed nice, and he was popular. And he happened to be like the first guy who tried to talk to me.

Mom wasn't wrong when she pointed that out, but I wasn't about to tell her so. Instead, I got all stupid about it and told her my group of friends all wanted to date him, but he chose me. She was not impressed at my half-lie. My friends all told me he was super cute and super sweet, and we were the cutest couple ever, but none of them had boyfriends. Once I had one, all they wanted to talk about was our makeout sessions.

"Go dance," Charlie says. His breath is in my ear. I can't think straight. I have to get away from him.

I shove my chair backward. "Okay."

Just as I'm out of my chair, a slow song comes on. Someone's big hand is on my waist. I resist the urge to bring him to his knees like I learned in self-defense class. My mom is huge on being an independent woman. I whip around. It's Sam. "Dance with me?"

"Where's Creed?"

"Why?"

I'm not about to out my best friend, and so I ignore the urge to shout out her name across the dance floor. "No reason. Sure. I'll dance with you."

Sam's hands are heavy on my waist. I suppose I should be thrilled that the most popular boy at Seeberger High wants to dance with me. But I know what the fascination is. I'm the new girl. "If you think I'm ignoring you to try to get your attention, you're wrong," I tell him.

He smirks like he knows how sexy he looks when he does it. The guy was born with good genes. I'll give him that. "That's not what I was thinking."

I hate being wrong. "Really? Then what were you thinking?"

He leans a little closer. I lean away. His shoulders droop. He relaxes his arms that felt like they were drawing me in. We scoot across the dance floor. "I was thinking that Charlie's my friend. And you better not break his heart."

My ears burn. My face flames. I know he's staring at me, but I can't look up. I'm not ready for him to see whatever truth lies there. "I'm not trying to," I mutter somewhere past his left shoulder. "We barely know each other."

He tugs at me. This time I let him pull me closer. I think he has more to say, and I don't want the rest of the dance floor to hear it. "It doesn't matter. Once Charlie makes up his mind about something, he rarely changes it. For whatever reason, he's stuck on you."

"But he's going off to college soon." I cling to my mother's words about guy's insulting girls to make them feel insecure so that they will be easier to manipulate. I wish Mom wasn't so jaded, but I also think she's right.

"I know. He has a full ride. You'd better not mess that up for him," he warns.

His words make me feel special, but they also piss me off. "Why is this all on me? I didn't ask for him to feel one way or the other about me," I argue. "I did nothing to make him think that I..."

"You're the first girl who's paid him any attention," he argues right back.

"I'm best friends with his sister. I'm in a Spanish project with him," I insist. "That's what we're doing here today. That's what this is." I stand so close, my chin is almost in his chest. I've yelled too many times today at this birthday party. I'm not doing it again. My eyes finally meet his. And whatever is going on between Charlie and me? It's none of this idiot's business.

"For real?"

I nod. "Yeah. For real. So if you'll excuse me, I need to start making videos so we can create a TikTok or a Reels for our grade. I don't want to mess it up," I snarl, throwing his warning in his face.

My phone vibrates in my back pocket. I reach for it and it throws me off balance in these boots that have just enough wedge to make me feel clumsy. I've never been good at walking in heels. I fall back into Sam, who catches me like it's nothing; like he didn't just save me from slamming my elbow into the concrete wall and possibly getting a hairline fracture. I've had one of those too. I'm not kidding when I say I'm the ultimate klutz. A picture of the invite I created earlier pops up on my screen.

"You sent me the invite. Thanks," I tell him with a smile.

A camera flash blinds me. "Awww. Sam caught Venus," Creed teases. *Crap balls.* Our situation probably looks a whole lot worse than it is.

I climb out of Sam's arms as quick as I can. "Thanks for catching me," I tell him as I scurry across the room. I can't believe I forgot about my Spanish project until now. Charlie stares at his half empty plates of food.

"I ate as much as I could, but it was too much," he explains.

I plop down in the chair beside him. "That's alright." I reach over and grip his knee. "Hey. We need to take a ton of pictures and make tons of short videos."

His eyes are glued to my hand on his knee. "Why?"

"Because it's for our project that I almost forgot." I say as I take my hand back. I can't believe I grabbed his knee, or that guys are so easy to mess with. "But we can still do this. So what we need to do is just take a ton and then we will review them later to make a video compilation," I tell him with complete confidence, like I have any idea what I'm talking about.

"Okay, sure." He stares at his phone. "But I'm not good with people."

I nod. "If you say so, but I think you do fine one-on-one." An awkward pause falls between us. Right now, I'm not a people person. "Anyway, why don't you take pictures of all the decorations. The food. Anything that doesn't require you talking."

He smiles at me. "Cool."

I give him a thumbs up. "Okay, cool. I'm just gonna go do my thing then." I look out at the dance floor. I'm super psyched there's so many people here, but it feels a bit over-whelming. It's easy to talk the talk, but getting it done? Where do I even begin? How am I going to get them to work with me to make a bunch of videos? The birthday girl pops into the corner of my eye. She's walking to the girl's bathroom. I chase after to get her permission.

She stands in front of the mirror, puckering her lips. "Excuse me, Cristina?"

"Yeah." She stares in the mirror.

I've never been as smooth of a talker as I pretend to be, and time is limited. I decide to lead with the truth. "So, we didn't just come here because we know Marti," I tell her.

She gives me the side-eye before returning to checking herself out in the mirror. The girl likes to primp.

"Why are you here, then? Is it because your friend is after my brother, because if she is, she can take a number. Santi has 'em waitin' in line."

"He's not that hot," falls out of my mouth before I can stop it.

Her hand flies to her hip and she faces me. The super chill attitude falls right in front of me. "I know, ri-ight? If they only knew what a *total nerd* he is, they wouldn't be fallin' for him left and right." She shakes her head. "It's just that pretty face of his that gets 'em. They can't see past his thick black hair, sad brown eyes, and full lips."

"Dude. He's your brother."

Her eyes widen. "Dude, I know. You think those sappy words came out of my mouth?"

"Uh, yeah. They kinda just did. I *literally* heard you say them."

She rolls her eyes. "I was just repeating what I heard some other girl say. Geez." She points a coffin nail at me. "So why are you here?"

I start to answer, but now I want to know. "Why do you say your brother's a nerd?"

"Um, because he like owns the box set of *Star Trek*."

I giggle. "I guess so, but Hans Solo is kind of hot. And I hate to admit it, but I love the name Luke Skywalker. It maybe retro, but it's still pretty cool."

She rolls her eyes. "Dude. That's *Star Wars*. I'm talking about *Star Trek*. The one that has its own language that's not real?" Her eyes search mine. I have no idea what she's talking about. She swats at the air. "Anyway, trust me. He's a huge nerd. Total Trekkie."

I giggle again. "I'll take your word for it."

She claps her hands. "So, why are you here?"

I blink twice as I try to gather my thoughts. "I'm here because I'm in a Spanish class at school. We have a big project due. I didn't have much time because I just joined the classroom. I moved in from out of state. So, Charlie and I are partners on this project. I went to the mall to find some Spanish-speaking people to practice English with for like job interviews and stuff, but Marti didn't have any candidates or whatever, so then Charlie asked her if there were any Spanish-speaking people anywhere that we might visit with, and she told us to come here."

"So you thought my quinceañera would fit your project," she says, "and you're not just here to see me."

I wish I could tell if she's upset, but her face is impassive. I force myself to look her in the eye. "Kind of, yeah." I sigh. "Mostly, yeah. I was thinking I could make some videos, take some pictures, and make like a video compilation of the event that I would use as a presentation to the class. I would send it to you, of course. If you like it, you can keep a copy or whatever."

"So you're like going to be my videographer free of charge."

I feel so professional. I nod like I totally know what I'm doing. I mean, I kind of know. I've done stuff like this at my old school in yearbook for like contests. I was pretty good on social media. "Yes."

"And I could put the word out if I like it?" she asks.

"Yes."

"Alright, cool," she answers before leaning into me, surprising me. She doesn't seem the type to act like a conspirator. "By the way, your guy is into you."

I can't believe how warm I feel at the thought of Charlie crushing on me. "Why do you say that?"

"Because he's always watching you, and the dude doesn't watch anyone. Trust me on that." Her eyes keep staring into mine. I want to look somewhere else. I feel like she sees too much. "Don't you like him?"

I shrug. "I could like him. It's just, he's a little intense. Not like scary intense, just...he's very into marine biology. He *really* likes the ocean."

She laughs. "What's wrong with a boy who knows his mind? At least he's not like into porn, or like weed, or like lots of girls."

"Guess I never thought about it like that."

She smacks my arm. "Sorry, I'm just saying. At least he's like honest with you about his feelings and not like so many guys who try to play it cool. They're after one thing, and once they get it, they kick you to the curb."

We step out from behind the panel. Her fingers are in her mouth. A loud whistle pierces my ear.

"Escuchame, ahora!" she hollers. "Venus, here, is my videographer. She's going to be making videos and taking pictures. Just do whatever she asks, okay?"

The music comes back on. She turns to me. "So, free services from you, and they better be good. I know a lot of people. Good or bad, your name will get around the quinceañera circuit."

Whoa. This is awesome. And scary. "Okay, cool."

She gives me a little shove. "That's it. That's all. Go, girl. Do your thing."

One hour and hundreds of pictures and videos later, I'm exhausted. "There has to be something in there somewhere worth keeping," I tell Charlie. "Because I can't take one more shot."

He hands me another pop. It's my fourth or fifth. I'm not sure. "You can't see it yet, Venus, but you will." He stares at the floor as we lean against the wall. "If we really can't come up with something, I'll tell Mrs. Hernandez how you single-handedly took one girl's super sad night and turned it into an epic birthday party she'll never forget."

I turn to him. He tugs at his collar like it's giving him hives. "You may not say much, Charlie, but when you do, it makes the rest of us sound so ordinary."

His head pops up. His eyes meet mine. "You could never be ordinary," he assures me before shoving off the wall with his foot. "Come on. She's about to cut the cake. Get your phone out. You don't want to miss it." Ugh. Maybe I can take one more shot, but I don't want to.

I fumble around my back pocket and shove my way through the crowd for the perfect shot while I try to forget the most wonderful five words anyone has ever said to me. I've only known Charlie for less than a week, but he already has a vice grip on my heart. How am I going to survive the rest of the school year if all we'll ever be is friends? But how can I love a boy who can't stand the thought of swapping spit with me? Has he never kissed a girl?

"Focus," I whisper to myself as Cristina's mom cuts into the gorgeous cake that could literally feed 300 people.

NINE

Charlie

It's the day after the quinceañera. We've gone over every video and every photo like five times. It's exhausting. I don't know how much more of this I can stand, even if it means I get to be near Venus and her floral notes. Her pale pink fingernails have strawberries on them, but they're like only part of the strawberry, and the impartiality drives me nuts. Why didn't they just do the whole strawberry?

"They're decals," she says.

"Excuse me?"

"My fingernails. They have decals."

I inspect them. "How do they get them so small?"

She shrugs beneath her soft blue hoodie that I know is soft because she insisted I touch the inside of her sleeve near her wrist. "I don't know. Maybe they have some sort of magic machine that shrinks everything down."

Her face is so serious, but she can't really believe that, can she? And if she can, what does that say about me? Could I really like a girl who is that gullible? "Who told you that?"

"Creed," she chokes. What is up with this girl?

"My sister told you that," I repeat, but I'm so confused.

She busts out laughing. "Dude. You make it so easy."

I want to laugh with her because I'm so relieved, but why does she keep trying to trick me? "I'm glad you find me so amusing," I mutter.

She shoulder bumps me. "Did you really think I'm so stupid I would believe there is a machine that shrinks *actual* strawberries into microscopic decals to stick on my fingers?"

I shrug. "You're the one who said it."

She rocks back and forth in her chair on wheels. "It would be kind of cool though. Like, if you could have a machine that lets you shoot a photo and then it automatically spits out the image as a decorative fingernail." Her mind is so weird.

"I would take pictures of clown fish," I offer.

She giggles and waves her pink fingernails again. "Yes. Because it is my absolute dream to wear decals of *clown fish* on my fingers." We sit here for a split second, just staring awkwardly at each other. Until she makes bug eyes at me. "The decals are from China. Give 'em enough time, and they can do anything."

Finally, something she says makes sense. "Yeah. You're probably right about that."

She leans back in her chair and looks away from me to look at the screen. "I think I need to look at the video again. It's missing something."

I groan as I continue to watch her. "Go ahead. I'm done looking at it. Change whatever you want. I'll take your word for it."

"Es muy bueno," she proclaims. "I'm just gonna add a few little green aliens here and there."

My eyes that are half-glazed from staring at the screen for like two hours too long pop open. "Excuse me?"

She nods. "Yeah. And maybe a few zombies with like bloody faces. We could make it like zombie apocalypse meets Roswell in the middle of a quinceañera."

She has to be joking. That's the dumbest idea I've ever heard, and if she were Creed, I'd tell her so. "I don't think that's a good idea. I don't think Cristina would like that."

She rolls her eyes. "Well, duh. We'll give Cristina a normal video. But after I add to it, I'll turn in the alien one to Mrs. Hernandez. She seems like she would totally go for sci-fi."

My stomach rolls. I can't let her do this, but how do I persuade her that it's a bad idea? "I guess I just didn't think that was the direction you wanted to go with this video. I think the polka music is great, and I like that you put all the captions in Spanish," I say, because Mom always tells me to look at the bright side.

She ducks. Her shoulders shake. Did I make her cry? Now what do I do? Do I reach out to her? Do I leave her alone? I hate this.

Her face comes up slowly. I want to look away. I hate it when girls cry. It makes me feel so helpless. Her hand is over her mouth, but I think she might be smiling. A tear rolls down her cheek. Why won't she say something? She falls back in her chair. "I so got you," she crows. "Two times in a row."

I feel so stupid. Creed says I can't tell what girls are thinking. I guess she's right.

"That was really mean," I tell her, because it was.

"It was just a joke," she scoffs.

"It wasn't funny. This is our grade," I cry.

"Whatever. It was *kind of* funny. You guys think you're the only ones who can pull pranks," she mutters. "I'm sorry you're so sensitive."

I'm an overly sensitive moron. I can't help it. Just like I can't help the fact my eyes are watering. I'm not crying in front of a girl. Especially the one I have a crush on. Why'd she have to be such a jerk to me? Twice, just like she said. I get up and walk out. If I say anything, I'll probably start blubbering.

"Forget girls," I mutter as I walk out of Venus's house. I have no idea where I'm going, but I don't care. I'm not staying. I'm so pissed. I was doing the best I could do to be polite even though Venus hadn't made a single change to the Spanish video for the past twenty-five minutes. I don't know how many times she needs to watch something before she decides it's fine. I could have told her it was fine half an hour ago. I think about everything that just happened between us. Where did it all go wrong? I was thinking about maybe asking her out, but then she had to go and make crap up just to see if I would believe it, and I believed it because she said it. Because I didn't think she would lie to me.

I was just trying to be nice, and I think she knew it, but she still had to be a jerk. Why did she think it was funny to trick me? Doesn't she know that's like the same as lying? Creed always tells me I'm too literal. If literal means expecting people not to lie to me, that's just common decency. And the video is perfect. I'm not in the habit of watching quinceañera videos, but I thought it was fantastic. I should have told her so. Maybe I should text her and tell her now. Or is it too late?

I sit down on a bench, take out my phone, and stare at it. Should I text her? What should I say? Should I say I'm sorry? But I'm not sorry. She should be sorry. She should say she's sorry for being so mean. My mind races. My heart pounds. Why isn't she texting me to tell me she's sorry?

Cars race by on the road in front of me, but I hardly notice them. I suppose I should tell Mom where I'm at, but I'm fricking eighteen years old. I don't need a babysitter. I just need someone to tell me how to talk to girls, or how to tell when they are joking. Or maybe I just need someone to tell me to lighten up. That's what Dad's always telling me. Well, at least he did until I told him I didn't like it, that his words had the opposite effect, that all they did was make me feel like an emotional wreck, at which point he looked so stricken I wish I had never said anything. I wished I would have just let him keep saying *lighten up* and I would just keep pushing those words into my head. It all floods within me like a tidal wave. I hate feeling this way, but I can't seem to stop. Like right now. I have the crazy urge to walk into oncoming traffic, for like a split second.

I wonder what it would feel like if a motorcyclist ran over the end of my foot. Would he wreck his bike? Or what if the corner of the Honda hit me in the knee? Would it just like blow out my kneecap or shatter my entire leg? And if it shattered my entire leg, would I like be disabled forever? And if I was disabled forever would that be better than being completely gone? If I were completely gone, my folks would be so sad, and I would never forgive myself. But if I'm not here, I guess I don't have the choice to forgive myself. Right? And what if I like stepped in front of a car and it didn't kill me but it messed up my brain and then I couldn't think the same way? Would I know it? Would I have moments where I remembered I used to be smarter, or would those moments disappear and then I wouldn't know until it happened again that I did know?

I close my eyes and count from forty-five to zero backward in threes.

I wish Venus would text me and apologize so I could walk back in her house to her perfect room that smells as good as she does. If I could just be there instead of here, I could stop having crazy, nonproductive thoughts. I stare at my blank phone screen, willing it to tell me something. Anything.

My fingers itch. I hate my choices. They all suck. I want more choices than sitting on a park bench like a loser still trying not to cry because I don't know what to do or how I feel other than knowing I probably pissed a girl off by walking out on our Spanish project. She's the first and only girl I've ever been interested in. I don't even know if we're in a fight or whatever, because we're not officially anything other than Spanish project partners. I'm only her partner because I couldn't stop stalking her. She didn't choose me. In fact, she unchose me. How lame is that? Venus is only my partner because Mrs. Hernandez told her she has to be. I close my eyes, pinch my nose, and will myself not to cry. This is so dumb.

This feels like every gym class I've had since fourth grade; the year I decided I would not care I was always picked last. My resolution to not give two shits would usually hold up until I stood all alone facing two groups of kids who did nothing to hide the fact they didn't want me. My betraying throat would tighten. My clueless eyes would water. My body did not agree with my mind. The latter knew that participating in team sports just because I'm a guy is stupid.

I don't know why athletic guys can't accept the fact that not every guy lives for competition and love of the game but can still like girls and be competitive in our own way if it's something we enjoy. Like, I'm pretty sure I can name all the species of trout in my state faster than any guy in my grade, even though I'm going to be a marine biologist and not an ichthyologist. And I could definitely win a *Who can be the quietest the longest* contest hands down any day of the week. I could live in a canoe for a week or longer by myself in the middle of a lake and be happy as a clam, as my grandpa would say.

Pondering my love for nature, I scroll through pictures of fish on my phone until I get to my drawings. My heart rate slows. My brain calms. I just need the familiar. My feelings for Venus are anything but. Whenever I'm around her, I can't stop looking. She has the nicest smile. Her eyes sparkle and shine. I think she enjoys talking to me. Or at least she did until today when we got in a sort of argument about her wanting to put zombies in the video. How was I supposed to know she was kidding? My stomach hurts. I'm stuck in a computer programming loop, but it's broken, and there's no outcome. There's just a regurgitation of emotions running through me. Over and over and over.

I should just get this misery over with and text her. Or I could text Creed and ask her what to say to Venus. Or I could text Creed and ask Creed if Venus has texted her about me. I shove my phone back in my pocket and lean back on the bench. I am not texting my sister to ask her what to do about being an idiot around her best friend. That's lame. That's even more lame than me sitting here on a bench wondering how to apologize to Venus when I don't feel like apologizing because I don't think I did anything wrong. She did.

I need someone to talk to, but my best friend is my sister, and my other best friend is Sam, who was all over Venus when he had her up against the wall, or she had him against the wall. I don't know. I was trying not to look once I saw them together. It hurt too much to watch. So I'm definitely not asking him what to say to her.

Having a crush on my sister's new friend sucks. It's a whole level of emotions I did not know I could have, and I'm pretty sure Tylenol or Ibuprofen won't make them go away. I can't ask my best friend about how to talk to my crush. I stare at the initials carved into the bench. Initials of normal people who have a girlfriend or boyfriend because they know how to talk to the person they like. Unlike me. I thought Venus liked me, but what if all this time she was just being nice to find out how weird I am? What if she felt sorry for me? What if she was laughing at me in her room because I'm so dumb I didn't know she was joking about the Spanish video? I wish I could hate her, or at least really, really not like her. That would be so much easier than this agony. I want to forget I ever knew her. Kind of.

But then I'd have to pretend I never saw the light in her eyes when she said my name for the first time. When *she* said it, *Charlie* sounded like a guy you'd like to meet, a guy you'd like to get to know because he's just like every other guy. He's normal and not an awkward introvert whose heart rate increases at the mere thought of going to a class keg party at the end of senior year at his best friend Sam's house because it's tradition.

When Venus looks at me, I forget I'm the gym class loser. I forget how the whole room got silent when I flew around the room like a turbo jet on steroids the day we had a substitute teacher, and she made us play with nature flashcards instead of multiplication. I was on cloud nine because everyone finally saw that I was good at something. But then Sam told me after school that day to turn down my weirdness dial or he couldn't be my friend anymore. From then on, I left my love for nature at home and tried to be more normal. Because if I didn't have Sam as a friend, I was pretty much on my own at school. Just like right now.

I should get up from this bench. But I can't. I'm not ready.

TEN

Venus

This is so stupid. I can't believe I'm driving around *illegally* looking for Mr. Pouty Pants who can't take a joke. Or two. So I told him a few whoppers to see if he would believe me. So what? Why is that such a huge deal? I'm the sophomore. He's a senior. If anything, he's supposed to torment me a little, not the other way around. My mind freezes on that word. *Torment*. It's not as bad as it sounds, right? I want to call Creed and whine to her about this, but I can't. Because he's her big brother. And then she would know I was getting all in angst about whatever this is, which is just stupid, because he's not even my boyfriend. He's my Spanish project partner. *The end*. And we are going to get a killer grade on this project. I just know it, which is what I will tell him as soon as I find him.

I could totally finish the video without him, the finishing song, roll the creds, etc., but it doesn't feel right. He needs to be there for it. Whether he wants to be or not, which is why I'm sitting in a line of cars at a stoplight in the middle of driving around in a town I still haven't entirely figured out while trying to creep on him through Snapchat location, which probably isn't the safest thing to do while driving. My head snaps up about the time I hear a honking somewhere near me. My car door opens at the same time I see his face. He gets in. "You better go before the guy behind you gets out of his car," he says.

I inch forward. "Where are you going?" he asks.

I glance in his direction. "I was in the middle of my project when someone ran out on me, and since you're my partner, I had to come and find you," I say before taking the first right so I can get away from whoever is riding my bumper. "And since this is not my hometown, I have no idea where I am."

He shifts in the passenger seat. "You're not supposed to be driving by yourself."

Ugh. This guy is so infuriating. I know that he knows he's being ridiculous, but his pride won't let him do anything but point out my flaws. "Well, you're eighteen, so I'm driving with an adult," I insist before giving him a side-eye that lingers enough to be insulting. "Technically."

He clears his throat. "Actually, I don't have a driver's license, so I'm not sure what the law says about that."

I know my eyes are popping, but seriously. "What do you mean you're not a licensed driver?"

He shrugs. "I don't have a license."

I smack the steering wheel. "Why?"

He turns away from me to look out the window. "I don't need one."

My eyes roll in my head before I can stop them. "Clearly," I get out.

His back stiffens in the corner of my eye. "What are you saying?"

I blink repeatedly in rapid succession. It's another thing I do when I'm stumped or irritated. Right now, I am both. How can a guy who has the brains to be a marine biologist be so clueless? "Dude. You got mad at me and walked out of my house, but you had no Exit plan. Like, were you just gonna walk the *fifteen miles* home?" I suppose I'm being cruel, but I really want to know what he's going to say.

"It's 12.7 miles," he replies.

I grit my teeth and consciously relax my jaw before I start grinding my teeth. "Are you seriously going to avoid answering my question by pointing out the exact distance, like that has any relevance to the point I was making, of which you are well aware."

He ducks. "You lied to me."

Which time pops into my head, and I stop my mouth before it comes flying out. Because he's right. And it makes me feel like crap. Did I date my last boyfriend so long that I didn't realize it's not okay to make stuff up just to see if someone will believe it? My face flushes when I recall how he used to make fun of me for believing him. Now here I am, doing the exact same thing to someone else. I'm not any different than the tool I left behind. This is not cool.

"I'm sorry," I say.

He fidgets with the door handle. I hate that he won't even look in my direction. "I mean it. I'm really sorry."

He lets out a sigh. "You going to turn around any time soon? If we keep going down this road, we'll be on the wrong side of Moscow."

I can't help it. Laughter pours out of me.

"I wasn't joking," he says.

I pull off into a side road leading to a cemetery. "I know, but you made it sound like we're in a movie," I say before stopping the car and looking at him with as serious of a face as I can make. "If we keep going down this road, we'll be on the wrong side of Moscow," I repeat to him in what I think is a dramatic, sinister voice.

He smiles full out, and I want to say it again. "I accept your apology," he says, and then we just sit here, staring.

"Can I, um..." Holy cow. I think he's going to ask to kiss me. I want him to. So bad. But something holds me back. It's not the right time.

"We need to get you a license," I blurt.

He startles before scooting toward the passenger door. "Okay."

My head swims. I make myself not look at his lips, but then he moves them, and my eyes are right back there. "I'm just saying that you can't go to college without a driver's license."

His hands grip the sides of his seat. "I know. It would be a lot easier to get on a plane if I had one."

"Have you ever driven a car?"

He shakes his head back and forth. "No."

"But Creed drives."

"Yeah."

"So she drives but you don't," I say like a broken record, but I'm just trying to understand.

He shrugs again. "Creed does a lot of things I don't do. Can we just go back to your house so we can finish the video please? I want to be done with it."

He sounds irritated. Is he upset because I interrupted him when he was going to try to kiss me? I think that's what was happening. I'm not about to ask. And if anyone should be irritated, it should be me, because I had to leave what I was doing and come looking for him. "Fine. Just let me enter my address into GPS on my phone."

Too many silent, awkward, minutes later, we're at the house. "How long will this take," he whines as we walk upstairs to my room.

I whip around from where I stand two steps above him. I can't believe he's being so demanding when he caused his own problem, which is what I'm about to tell him, until I see the longing written all over his face. Something takes over me. My hand is on his collar. I'm moving in slow motion as the rest of me follows the path of my hand. I clumsily bump into him. His hand goes to my waist, but it feels totally different than when Sam's hand was there.

Charlie's hand rests just above my hip. His touch is so light it's almost like it's not there, but then his fingers move just enough to touch skin, and it zings me clear down to my toes. How does one simple movement from this strange, awkward guy hit me like a bolt of lightning? I'm stunned and disoriented. I'm so close, all I see is one side of his nose, the hint of a dimple, and the side of his perfect chin. He's gone quiet on me. I wish he would say something – anything to remind me of how different we are and that it would be the worst idea for me to start something with him, no matter how good his touch feels.

"Your hand is on my collar," he scolds, and that's it. That's the last straw.

My lips find his. If he can shock me with his hands, I'll shock him right back. At least that's what I told myself as I lean in to shut the mouth of mister overly sensitive know-it-all who makes me feel like a terrible person half the time, including now. What am I doing kissing a guy I don't have any intentions of dating? I back away as fast as I went in. His eyes are still closed. I'm torn between going back for more or going to my room. His hand is still on my waist. "Hey."

"What," he says, but his eyes remain closed.

"Open your eyes," I almost bark.

He ducks and nips in his bottom lip just enough to get me going all over again. It's a totally hot Miles Teller move from *The Spectacular Now*, one of my favorite movies. "No."

If this moment weren't so strange and awkward, I could almost giggle. "I don't—"

"If I open my eyes the most perfect moment I've ever had is gone," he says in a voice so quiet I almost don't hear him. He opens his eyes. And now we stare at each other like a couple in a black-and-white silent movie standing on the railroad tracks while the train bears down on us, but we're too terrified to move even though not moving means certain death.

"What?" he whispers.

I open my mouth to answer. *That's the most beautiful thing a guy has ever told me. Your honesty brings me to my knees. I'm not sure I feel any part of myself at this exact moment in time. Will you be my secret boyfriend because dating you would crush any chance I have at being halfway cool?* I think he's waiting for me to speak.

"Let go of my shirt," I say just as quiet.

"I don't want to."

Well. That was unexpected, unoffensive, and possibly hotter than his lips. I think I might melt on my own stairs. "Excuse me?" I say instead of telling him every delicious thought that just ran through my head.

He lets go of me like I'm a hot stove. I turn away from him and take two more steps to the second story before turning left to go down the hallway to my room. "For the record, you grabbed my shirt first," he calls. I keep walking.

His footsteps grow louder. I want to shut the door in his stupid, persistent face, but I can't. Because he's not confident as his truthful words make him sound. He's literal. He's brutally honest. He's socially awkward. He's a stubborn ass. But he's not arrogant. He doesn't know how to be.

By the time he steps in my room, I have the quinceañera video pulled up again. "So we need to pick a song to play while the credits roll."

"You mean my name and yours," he says, and he sounds so pleased.

"Yes, but it's not as short as that. There's like all of our titles."

"Titles?" he asks.

"Yes. There's film producer, film editor, videographer, music production," I pause while my brain tries to think of more things.

"But those are all you," he argues.

"Yeah, so?"

"So are you literally going to list your name after each title?"

I nod and smile. "Yes. That is the way things are done in the real world."

"Won't that look silly?"

I shake my head back and forth. "No. It will make our video look more official. It will make it stand out. It will show Mrs. Hernandez that we took this assignment seriously," I say as I spin in slow circles on my swiveling office chair. "I am also the *queen* of mundane titles that basically mean the same thing," I say as I stare at the ceiling. "That is part of the fun of creating."

"And you like to see your name multiple times," he comments, but he sounds too curious to sound critical.

"Maybe," I say as I smile while hanging my head over the back of my chair before turning to look at him and point in his general direction. "But you have to pick out the song for the credits."

"With your approval," he answers.

"This is a joint project," I reply.

ELEVEN

Charlie

Venus makes me stand up in front of the whole class while she presents our Spanish project to the class. She does an amazing job with the speech she says we wrote together; if me listening to her read every sentence of the twenty-five sentences she wrote multiple times until I couldn't take it anymore and told her I had to go the restroom because I thought I was coming down with the stomach flu constitutes being a contributing editor. So while she stands in front of the class glancing at her notecards in between pausing and looking over at me as if to silently ask if I have anything to say and looking as beautiful as what I imagine an undiscovered species will look someday when I find one, I focus on my not locking my knees so I won't faint.

In between my glances at her, I stare at the clock on the back wall so I won't have to look any classmate in the eye. The second hand has gone full circle ten times, but it feels like it should have been like fifty. That's how tortured I feel. Although I'm a senior, this is the first time I've had to stand in front of a group. Every teacher in this building is well aware of my phobia of doing exactly what I'm doing now.

The music continues to play. It feels like forever. Just when I think I can't take it any longer and I'm prepared to tell Mrs. Hernandez I feel a bout of explosive diarrhea coming on, the music stops, and clapping begins. Venus bows. I would bow, but I'm sort of frozen. I want to sit in my chair, but my legs don't want to move. And so I stand here like a flat-faced stick boy in child's drawing. "Charlie," Mrs. Hernandez says from somewhere behind me. "Did you have something to add?"

Nothing helpful. "I, um..., well, I..."

"Charlie was just going to tell you how he chose the totally amazing song that tied the entire video together," Venus prompts from where she sits while smiling so big I think her face might crack. "While he goes to his seat," she continues in a slightly quieter voice.

Her commands get my feet moving. "Right. That's right, I'm just going to do that," I say as I slip into my desk and let out the breath I feel like I've been holding since Venus started talking eleven minutes ago.

"The song," Venus growls at me from two rows over.

"Yes. The song," I answer in a loud voice. "So I chose the song that Venus told me to choose after I chose seven songs she did not like," I answer, at which point Venus buries her face in her crossed arms so it doesn't hit the desk.

Mrs. Hernandez laughs. "Well, it sounds like the two of you put a lot of effort into this video, but it was a little on the short side."

I feel terrible. "It would have been longer, but I made Venus take part of it out because I didn't want to be in it," I insist. "That's why it was too short."

Mrs. Hernandez stares at me. "Oh?"

"Yes. And also, you should know that the girl's birthday was a complete disaster. There was no one there. The band's van broke down so she had no music. Half her family was sick and they could not come. The other half had no way to get there. Her parents had all this wonderful food, but no one was going to eat it," I explain before pointing to Venus. "And I had to dance with the birthday girl because she was crying, and I'm a terrible dancer, and then someone filmed it and sent it to Venus, but I begged her not to put it in the video because I don't like being on camera."

She crosses her arms. "Well. That sounds like quite the fiasco."
I nod. "It would have been if Venus hadn't sent out the invites by Snapchat and social media. She got all the people there."

Mrs. Hernandez's eyes widen. "Is this true?"

I look over at Venus, whose face has not moved from staring into her desk. "Yes," she kind of groans. "You *know Charlie*. He cannot tell a lie," she continues, but it doesn't sound like a compliment.

"I still don't know why that's such a bad thing," I reply before turning to look at Mrs. Hernandez once more. "So really, it's a good thing we crashed this girl's party, because otherwise, there would have been no one there."

Mrs. Hernandez coughs. "You crashed her party, as in you weren't invited."

I shake my head again. "Technically we were invited, because Venus got the invite from the lady at the learning center at the mall. She took it from her purse."

Mrs. Hernandez's eyes get big again. She must be easily surprised. "You *stole* something from someone's purse?"

I consider her question for a second or two and mostly ignore the strange noises coming from Venus. "No. I don't think so. The lady was standing right there. She told us she didn't want to go and that we could go, and she was going to maybe give the invite to us, but Venus grabbed it before the lady named Marti could decide, so I'm not sure."

My teacher shakes her head. "This story just gets crazier and crazier."

I tap my fingers on my desktop. "I know. After Venus does all this for this girl named Cristina, Cristina tells her she's putting the video we make out on TikTok and Reels for the quinceañera circuit, so Venus better do it right, or else her reputation as a videographer is not going to be good."

Mrs. Hernandez stands up from behind her desk. I can't tell from the dazed look on her face what is going on inside her head. "So, let me get this straight. You stole an invite. You crashed a party. You then invited a bunch of kids that this girl didn't know, and you danced with the birthday girl because she was *crying*? And now your name is circulating the quinceañera circuit because you made it into a TikTok?" She sounds a little excited. She claps her hands. "Do you not see what you've done?"

Venus's head comes off her arms to look at the teacher. "Made complete and total fools of ourselves for an ungrateful spoiled birthday girl?"

Mrs. Hernandez laughs again. She's in a great mood. "No," she exclaims. "You've taken a simple Spanish project and transposed it into something real, something of value, something..." she snaps her fingers and points a finger at me and one at Venus. "You two could totally enter the entrepreneurial contest with this! That's what you should do."

"We don't even have a calling card or logo or whatever," Venus protests. "And he's going to graduate at the end of this year, and then it would just be me."

"Then bring his little sister into it. She's your friend," Mrs. Hernandez argues.

"That's nepotism," I say. I'm not so sure I can work with Creed on anything, especially if finances are involved.

"Dude. Chillax," Venus says to me. "I'll handle the hard stuff."

I look up at Mrs. Hernandez. "Is us creating a real business part of our grade?"

Her eyes light up for half a second. "That's not a bad idea, but no. That wouldn't be fair to the rest of the class, because I didn't make it a requirement in the outline for the project." She sits back down and leans forward on her desk. "But, if you want some extra credit, I would definitely consider that possibility."

I sit back in my chair. What have I gotten myself into? All I wanted was to be in the same classroom with Venus, and now I'm making music videos, becoming some kind of TikTok creator, and considering running some sort of business I have no business running. I look over at Venus one more time. Is all of this trouble worth being near her so I can breathe in her space? She makes goofy bug eyes at me before giving me a small smile and tilting her head to the side just a little. *Dang it. She totally is worth the trouble.*

She turns away from me to stare straight ahead like she didn't just decimate me to smithereens in my chair. One small curve of her lip on its way to a smile reminds me of our kiss, the only kiss I've ever had, the only kiss I ever want to have. Because it was so perfect. What if I kiss another girl and it's terrible? What if it erases my memories of being electrified from my head to my toes, but in a good way. Like what I imagine it would feel like if I could feel every molecule in my body buzzing with uncontained excitement and joy all at the same time but also separately as the touch of her lips to mine knocked me down like dominoes. It's as if I felt my neurons pinging off every nerve ending as they zipped around inside me. It was the most wonderful feeling in the world. Why would I want to ruin it?

The bell rings. "Looks like you're stuck with me, Charlie," Venus says as I walk beside her through the doorway.

"Yeah," I reply. "I guess so."

"Well, if you don't want to be," she says. She sounds kind of nervous, but her words excite me. She's giving me an out. I would be a fool not to take it. She must have some clue of how terrible I'll screw up if I'm her partner on stage. It would only end in disaster.

I bet she'd rather work with Creed. That makes perfect sense. Anybody in this school would choose my sister over me, and with good reason. Creed may be a bit opinionated and hard to take, but she's still a lot easier to work with.

"You could work with Creed," I offer. How did I get to her locker? Why am I not at mine?

"If that's what you want," she says. I don't think she sounds exactly happy about it, but I'm not sure.

What'd I do now? "Well, it's whatever you want. I mean, I'll be graduating soon, and..." I stop talking. I have no idea what to say. She looks like she might cry. I clear my throat. "Well, I've got to get to class. Just think about it and let me know. I won't say anything to Creed. I mean, it's your call." I'm a bumbling idiot. What is going on? She doesn't answer, and so I hurry away.

A week goes by, and then two. I haven't heard much from Venus in person since I ran away from her like a scared little b—, at least that's what Creed would say. I prefer the term nonconfrontational. There's nothing wrong with that personality trait, which is the whole reason I haven't said a word to Venus about the entrepreneurial contest which is today; a fact I remember as I walk into Spanish and see Mrs. H's poster about it. *Great. I'm going to have to sit through the assembly with all the other students knowing Venus is somewhere in the crowd and she's mad at me.*

"I was sorry to hear you two had withdrawn from the entrepreneurial contest," Mrs. Hernandez says as soon as I sit down.

What the heck is she talking about? We never entered. Unless Venus did and didn't tell me because she hoped I would come around. I knew nothing about this. I scan the room frantically for Venus. She's nowhere. "Oh, yeah," I reply because I don't know what to say.

"Your video seemed pretty tight to me, but Venus mentioned there were a few things she'd like to tweak before putting her name on it as a professional."

I nod. I have no idea what to say. "Yeah."

"Being a perfectionist is good, Charlie, unless it gets in the way of a person ever finishing anything. There's a fine line between perfection and leaving everything undone."

"There is," I agree again. *Where the heck is Venus?*

"Well, please tell her I missed seeing her today."

"Okay," I say. *Wait, what? Where is she?*

Mrs. H stares at me. It's making me feel weird. "If you change your mind about the contest, you can still enter," she prompts.

"Uh huh," I mutter beneath my breath.

The rest of Spanish class is lost on me. All I can think about is where Venus is if she's not here. Is she okay? Did something happen to her? Is she sick? She never misses class. Her absence is so annoying. I think I just failed my pop quiz. I'm pretty sure one-word answers are not what Mrs. Hernandez was looking for as I hand in my paper and walk through the door. "Charlie," Mrs. H. says to me as I step out into the hallway.

"Charlie. You can't walk out in the middle of class," Mrs. H whispers as she stands in her doorway with her back to the class.

I look down at my watch. I feel so lost. *Where is Venus?* "I'm sorry. I have to know where she is."

She frowns. "I understand how you think you feel about this girl, but you can't just ignore my schedule," she scolds.

I blink. "Of course. What was I thinking," I say to her as I follow her back into the Spanish classroom. "I'm so sorry," I say.

"I know you are," she answers. "Go ahead and take a seat so you can stare at the clock for the next twenty-two minutes," she says with another small smile. "It's obvious you won't be getting any work done today."

I stare at the top of my desk in confusion. Our video didn't need tweaking. It was freaking Harry Styles perfect. Venus said so. Many times. When she was trying to convince me to enter the contest with her. She told me she would pick out our clothes, the color scheme for the background, and give me a few lines because she would be doing most of the talking.

"All I had to do was stand there and answer a few questions. Surely, I could do that, right?" she'd said.

I hated feeling so dumb around her, but the thought of standing in front of the entire school plus a panel of judges plus getting my picture taken was all too much. But at the same time, I couldn't tell her the only reason I had done any of it was because of her. That's it. That's all I had to say, and I couldn't. So now I've ruined her chances at winning a contest. I'm the worst.

My stomach hurts. My head aches. Why did Mrs. H. tell me something I didn't need to know when Venus isn't here for me to talk to her about it? And why didn't Venus take Creed as a partner instead? I told her she could. I get out our video we made together and watch it again on mute. I can't believe what I might be about to do.

TWELVE

Venus

I woke up with the flu. I barely got to the toilet before the bile hit the back of my throat, sending me straight out of bed like a cannonball as I shot down the hallway with my hand over my mouth to hold in the trail of acid my body was determined to generate from everywhere repeatedly. I ended up sitting on the toilet, leaning over the wastebasket. I've never been this sick in my life. I felt like I wanted to die.

After spending most of the day on the bathroom floor and feeling like an alien took over my body, I finally settled down enough to text Creed.

VENUS:

I'm sick. Stomach bug. It's the worst. I'm sorry. I'll see you in a few days. -V

CREED:

Ugh.

VENUS:

Yep.

CREED:

> This must be why my idiotic brother is mentally crapping himself behind the mic at the entrepreneurial contest.

VENUS:

> What? We aren't doing the contest. He said he didn't want to.

Creed: I'm not lying. I'm sitting here. Watching him making a complete fool of himself. He got through the video okay since he didn't have to speak. And then he somehow turned what should have been a two-minute speech into six painful minutes of I don't even know what he said. I was too distracted by him bobbing and weaving with the mic. It looked like a one-sided drunken boxing match. Now he's on the Q&A. It's a little better except for the fact that I think he's seconds from passing out.

Her brutally honest no-holds-barred description of Charlie that I can only forgive because she's his sister and she has no idea how I feel about him makes me want to cry. And it's not just because I'm already feeling like someone's literally squeezing the crap out of my stomach that won't stop cramping.

VENUS:

> Oh, no.

CREED:

> Oh, yeah. It's hilarious.

VENUS:

> I think I'm going to be sick.

CREED:

> Yep. It's pretty horrific.

VENUS:

> No. Like literally sick. I'm sorry. I have to go.

I put the phone out of reach before everything comes at me in waves. This is the worst. Whoever thinks taking pills to make you crap 24/7 to lose weight is insane. I'm so glad no one is here to hear me. I probably sound like a blue whale in labor.

Minutes later, I wipe the sweat from my forehead, rinse my mouth out with water, and pop a mint.

CREED:

> I have no idea why he thought this was a good idea. This is like his worst nightmare. He hates being in front of crowds. I have no idea why he would do this to himself.

I close my eyes and lay down in the fetal position on my bathroom floor. "Because of me," I moan to myself. There's no way I'm telling Creed. I clutch my phone in the palm of my hand and wish for tomorrow as I lay with my back to the offending trash can that I'll have to empty before Mom comes home. I am so done. I hope my body figures out there's nothing left for it to purge. I reach for my phone.

VENUS:

> Maybe he wanted to try something new.

CREED:

> I guess. But he really doesn't need to be skilled at public speaking to be a marine biologist.

"It wouldn't hurt. If he like has to do presentations to get funding for projects he's sure to be doing," I murmur into the tile floor. I don't have the heart or the energy to argue with my best friend who can't find out I'm seriously crushing on her brother right now. Why does he keep torturing himself like this?

"Venus?"

Mom's home. This thought registers in my brain about the time the bathroom door flies open. "Honey. Are you okay?"

I stare at her through glazed eyes. "I have the flu."

"Why didn't they call me?" she demands.

"I might have called them myself from our landline," I tell her. "You mentioned you were going to be in meetings all day. I didn't want them to interrupt your day, so I just said I was you."

Her slightly narrowed eyes soften. "Oh, Venus. I'm so sorry. I would have taken the call from your school. What can I get you?"

My stomach cramps again. "A new stomach," I manage before I pick myself up off the floor, shut the door with my foot, and kneel as I grab the sides of the toilet. I feel demented as I smile over Creed's texts about her brother humiliating himself just to make me happy. *What is wrong with me*, I wonder just before I dry heave repeatedly.

When it's over, I lay back on the bathroom tile with my phone.

VENUS:

> Mom. I would like Sprite and peppermints please pretty please. And whatever else you think I would like after I am done throwing up. Thank you.

I take a selfie to send to Charlie, telling myself I'm sending it so he knows why I'm not there.

VENUS:

> I thought we agreed not to enter the contest.

CHARLIE:

> I didn't know you entered it. Why didn't you tell me?

My stomach churns, but for a different reason. I can't believe how mad I've been at him for the past two weeks, or how bad I've been giving him the cold shoulder. There's no way to tell him I wish he would have asked but he didn't, and if he had asked, he would have known, without sounding a little crazy. I know he can't read my mind, but he'd have to be completely dense to not know that I really wanted to do this contest. And I wanted to do it with him.

VENUS:

Must have slipped my mind.

CHARLIE:

You forgot you entered us both in a contest and also forgot to tell me?

Yep, I'm officially nuts.

VENUS:

Guess so.

CHARLIE:

I think you are not telling the truth.

VENUS:

I think you are dancing with death. Skull emoji.

CHARLIE:

If Mrs. H. had not told me today that you did all this, I never would have known and I would not have reentered the contest.

He's so irritating. Why is he so bent on making me tell him that I did something without telling him? I obviously wasn't going to go through with it which is why I backed out at the last minute. He's the one who made it weird by reentering.

VENUS:

F I N E. I entered our names in the contest. You did not change your mind. I withdrew our names from the contest. No harm. No foul.

CHARLIE:

I don't think it's fair that you entered me in
something and then took me out. That makes
me look like a quitter.

VENUS:

Really? That's what you're upset about? The
judges who have no idea who you are would
think you're a quitter. Eye roll emoji.

CHARLIE:

I don't know. Maybe.

VENUS:

If this is your way of apologizing for backing
out on an invitation I extended to you and not
your sister which would indicate I clearly
wanted you to be my partner and not the
latter, I accept it. But only because I can't
believe you stood up in front of the entire
school.

My fingers fly, but they can't fly fast enough. It is a lengthy
explanation which I immediately regret, but I send it anyway.

CHARLIE:

I believe we established it was important to
you. I do not understand why you are upset
with me. I did something I hate to do because
you wanted it done.

Ugh. This boy is incredibly dense when it comes to reading
between the lines. I all but told him I have a mega crush on him—
one I do not want to have.

VENUS:

I wasn't even there! You can't blame me for
this.

CHARLIE:

Who said I was blaming you? I told you to ask Creed. She's so much better at this stuff. She would have gotten you a better grade, I am sure.

I should drop it. He's clearly not getting my point. I feel like a broken record. But I have to have the last word. Or maybe on some sick level I don't want to contemplate, I am enjoying this argument a little too much.

VENUS:

You and I made the videos together. This was our project. This was our thing. It makes perfect sense that we would do the presentation.

CHARLIE:

Okay, fine. I'm done arguing. The presentation is done. It was more mortifying than watching two octopi mate. But I did it.

Well. That disturbing vision came completely out of left field, and I am googling it right now.

VENUS:

Ew. Gross. You did that?

CHARLIE:

Which one? I've done both.

VENUS:

Um, why?

CHARLIE

Research.

VENUS:

You don't need to see it to know it happened.
The octopi population is not going extinct.
Obviously, they procreate. Somewhere in the
deep sea where no one sees because that's
the way it should be. I think I just threw up in
my mouth. Stomach flu is the worst.

I type and send right before clicking on the video, which I close half a second later. Watching octopi procreate while having the stomach flu is not one of the best ideas I've ever had.

I turn to the side and spit in the toilet.

CHARLIE:

If it makes you feel any better I threw up in the
bathroom five minutes before I gave our
presentation.

I giggle at the thought.

VENUS:

It does.

CHARLIE:

You really are a sadist.

VENUS:

Whatevs. I will say this, you're a little crazy,
but in a good way.

CHARLIE:

Crap balls. I am. I didn't even think about the
impact my performance will have on our
grade.

VENUS:

Chillax, Charlie. It can't be anything but
positive.

I send my heartfelt encouragement to him and hope I'm right. I'm 89 percent sure I believe what I say. Mrs. H. wouldn't be that cold, not when she's the one who told us to enter the contest.

What worries me is our kiss. I kissed him, but he kissed me back. And ever since that kiss, he's been acting really weird. I think. I don't know.

I've only kissed one other guy, and he took it like an invitation for him to practically attack me every time we were alone. I blush at the thought. It was fun making out with my ex, but when it became everything we ever did the excitement of having a boyfriend wore off. He never wanted to just talk. Or hang out. Or laugh and joke. Like we were never friends.

Charlie and I could be great friends, save for the fact that his sister is my best friend and I don't think she'd appreciate that I kind of find myself Snapping Charlie as much as I Snap her. There's also the constant underlying tension between Charlie and I that some sick part of me finds way too exciting. I love knowing that we kissed, and that I don't know what comes next, but I hate how it makes me feel when I'm not sure I'm ready to date him in public, if that was an option. He's just so literal. And awkward. And introverted. And so comfortable with all of it. I don't know any other senior who attends regular classes and wears Ocean Life T-shirts every day.

He doesn't have a single item of clothing that doesn't have to do with his love of the ocean, plant life, or strange creatures of the deep. To be fair, I follow some besties on Instagram and TikTok who are like serial Taylor Swift fans. They've been to so many of her concerts and if I didn't know better, I'd swear they've been robbing banks on the side to fund their obsession with being Swifties. Every post they put out there is tied to her. Everything in their closets has something to do with her. I know because they made a TikTok about that too. I was fascinated and frightened all at the same time. Taylor Swift covered every inch of every shelf, wall, and carpet area beneath the bright shine of a single light bulb as I stepped into their social media shrine at 3 a.m. when I could not turn off the TikTok.

I guess if I looked at it that way, at least he's academically obsessed. It's not like anyone's worried about him chasing down a blue whale with a giant harpoon like some crazed, murderous, obsessive fan. His goal is to discover a new species and save the ocean. I think. Which to me seems like a daunting task. I have no idea what I want to be when I grow up. I can't even decide if I want to be someone's girlfriend even though he's an incredibly good kisser and a lot less handsy than my last boyfriend. And he's really good at Snapchat. He responds right away. And he's funny. And he's cute. And he loves sending me Selfies of his shoelaces that have the most amazingly detailed microscopic turtles and dolphins drawn on them cause he's a crazy-good artist.

I wish I could share all these terrific attributes with my best friend about my crush that grows harder to ignore by the message, but I can't. I'm sure his sister doesn't want to hear me salivating over her big brother. And so I have no choice but to keep them in a pocket inside my brain and shove it way down deep every time I see green-eyed Charlie with his messy hair, lopsided grin, and intense stare which is usually buried in a book. I can't believe I'm falling for a studious, conflicted boy with an unfiltered mouth that tells his every feeling, especially after we've kissed.

THIRTEEN

Charlie

"Yo, Char-lie," Sam barks in my ear just before flopping down on the floor beside where I sit beneath my locker in my designated hall space. His space is actually seven lockers down, but Sam does not adhere to the unspoken code of ethics that allows me to sit amongst my peers as if I were an accepted member of the hallway species, which I clearly am not, except for times like right now.

"Yes," I say as I stare at my latest Amazon purchase, an updated Brittanica encyclopedia that contains 3D pictures of every species of clown fish in even greater detail. I am enthralled.

His offending hand closes my book. "Yo, check out my new sneaks. They're so tight. Got 'em last weekend when I was out with Keersten." He elbows me in the ribs. "We had some fun, if you know what I'm sayin'."

His tone tells me he and Keersten smashed, but I'm not about to ask. "Cool," I tell him instead, while hoping he will not elaborate on his bedroom activities.

"Yeah, so anyway, my parental units are going away on some corporate cruise thing of my dad's, so I have the house all to myself," he says as he drops a flyer into the middle of my book. I snatch it up. The ink is so colorful it still looks wet. I will be seriously PO'd if his entertainment leaves a stain on my brand-new book. "You in or out, man."

My eyes scan the date. Two weeks from now. Is that a short enough time frame for me to say I can't come because I didn't get enough notice? "I don't know," I say as I steal a glance in his direction to gage his response to my uncertainty, but his attention is on the hallway.

My sister hovers. Her eyes are glued to the flyer in my hand. I think this is not good. Her eyes are usually glued to Sam's face. I can't believe that I wish they were right now. "Hi Charlie," Venus says so quiet I almost don't hear her.

"Hey," I say, but my eyes are mostly on Creed, who won't stop staring at the flyer.

"Hey, Creed," Sam says. "What's up."

Creed flashes him a smile, the one I never see at home, but that's okay. It creeps me out. "Hey, Sam. What's up with you," she parrots in a weird little voice. I want out of this conversation. Now.

He hands her a flyer. "Here. I'm having a party. Keep it on the down low, though, got it? It's upperclassmen only, but I'll make an exception for you two, but only if you bring your brother. He needs to live a little."

Her eyes widen. I recognize that look. She's totally doing a Beyoncé dance inside her head. "Yeah, okay. Sounds chill," she says before slipping her hand through Venus's arm and walking away.

"And bring your friend," he hollers as he watches them walk away.

"Dude," I say. "That's my sister."

"Yeah, she's hot," some guy who sat down on the other side of Sam sometime between the beginning and end of our conversation that I don't want to be having. "And so is her friend."

"I don't know," Sam says. "I don't date my friend's sisters, and her friend is a little overly opinionated and colorful," he adds. And I relax. "But a little spice is fun too," he jokes before giving me an ornery grin. "I like a challenge."

Sam stands up, and so does his friend. He kicks my shoe with his foot. "See ya, later, Charlie. You're totally coming to my party." He says with a wink.

Images of harpooning Sam and his stupid friend flood my mind. I wonder if one spear could pierce both their bellies just like I wonder how fast they'd bleed out on the boat before I threw them overboard. I duck and turn to the Tomato clown fish. It's so hard having a crush on a girl. I never thought I would imagine killing my best friend just because he's a major player and he made a joke about hitting on her.

My head aches when I try to figure out if Sam meant anything that he said or if he was just kidding like he usually does just to see if I will react. I don't know. He doesn't seem like he would go after my sister, but Venus is her friend, so there's nothing about her that makes *her* off-limits to Sam. If he wants to be with Venus, he will. And there's nothing I can do about it.

My joy over Venus saying hi to me mere seconds ago disappears as quickly as it filled me. I hate Mondays. I hate parties. I hate high school. The bell rings. I slide my new book into my backpack and grab my advanced chemistry book before jogging off to class. I also hate being tardy.

The best thing about advanced classes is their sole focus is on learning, and they're a great excuse to stop thinking about how to get out of going to Sam Birk's stupid epic party, but I can't seem to stop obsessing over the laws of attraction and how to fight them. If I don't go to the party, Creed doesn't go, and if Creed doesn't go, Venus won't go. If Venus doesn't go to Sam Birk's house, it decreases the possibility greatly that she could end up in his bed. No girl I ever knew invited to smash with Sam turned him down.

"Facts," I mouth to myself with determination as I plop my butt in the back row. I just need to figure out all the elements that would allow Creed to go to this stupid party and then systematically eliminate them.

1. My parents love Sam, but they don't want Creed going to the party unless I go because of her age.

2. My parents are party people. They'll be super excited that I am invited to Sam's party. I know this because my mother mentioned Sam's party to me last year and I didn't have the heart to tell her I wasn't going, and so I sort of insinuated I wasn't invited, which was the worst idea because she then threatened to call his mother. I then had to beg her for half an hour not to call anyone and endure her tears and headshaking over the fact that my best friend did not invite me to a major social event. I had to pretend I was so hurt that I didn't want to talk about it, and that even though Sam hurt my feelings, and I'm a guy, I would talk to him about it. We would work it out. Mom did not need to get involved. It was one of the most painful hours of my life.
3. If Creed is with me, she doesn't have a curfew.
4. All of our cars have GPS capability. It is impossible for them to get lost (on the way to a party).
5. As long as the car has the same amount of gas it did when it left the house, Mom and Dad do not care where we go.
6. Mom and Dad love Venus. They trust her. They think she is good for Creed.
7. Mom and Dad would be thrilled if I went to a high school party.
8. Sam's parents don't know he's throwing a party.

My fingers tremble as I write number eight. Sam is my best friend. Am I willing to throw him under the bus just so he won't hit on Venus at his epic party. Yes, I totally would as a last resort. I really don't want to. But when I think of him looking at her like he looks at so many other girls, I want to straight-up murder him and his hot face, his killer smile, and his magical eyes that make girls throw themselves at him in wild abandon.

Sam and his natural attraction to the female species reminds me of migrating female salmon who swim upstream for miles and miles just to have a little fun before they die. Getting to their destination takes so much time and energy, once they get what they're after they're exhausted, and they have nothing more to give. Every girl Sam has ever been with must know their relationship is dead in the water, but they still choose to walk into his lair. And that's fine, so long as Venus walks into my lair. I don't want all the girls in the sea; I just want one.

I tap my pencil as I read over the first list in order to make a second one. In order to counteract this list, I just have to:

1. Make my parents not like Sam
2. Not let them find out about the party.
3. Convince them to instill a curfew for Creed.
4. Deactivate the GPS in all the cars.
5. Steal Creed's money so she can't put gas in the car.
6. Make Dad and Mom doubt Venus is a good influence.
7. Not let Mom and Dad know about the party.
8. If all else fails, tell Sam's parents he's having a party.

Who knew having a crush on one girl could be so complicated?

FOURTEEN

Venus

"Can you believe it?" Creed squeals in my right ear. Her shrill voice echoes off the bathroom walls, splintering my eardrums. "We're invited to Sam's party." Her big baby blues that I didn't think could get any wider, start buggin'. Creed with her metallic green eyeshadow, continually wet lip gloss, lacy grey sweater, blue velvet shirt, and skinny black jeans slightly resembles the spot-on dragonfly Sam was coloring the other day while I was at her house. He was hovering, as usual, in a chair with his sketch pad and his headphones, looking all cool and chill, like a tortured artist with his sole focus on yet another killer drawing of lake life that is an exact replica of the real deal, but without the grimy, slimy pond water that I am so not a fan of. I'd wade through Charlie's colored pencil version of a lake any day of the week. He's so fire.

"I'm tell-ing you, this party is going to be so vibin', you won't believe it," she implores as she grabs my arm. I step out of my daydream of Sam and his beautiful face of concentration and reorient to the present; Creed screeching in my ear. My stomach churns at the thought of what we will be walking into – a party full of upperclassmen drunk off their stupid butts. I think I like parties. I've been to a few. But something tells me this party will be different. I've never known anyone whose parents go on corporate cruises, so I can only imagine the size of Sam's house. He probably lives in a gated community. His parents probably own the biggest house that sits on the highest hill.

And maybe that bothers me more than it should. It's not Sam's fault his parents have money. He's not really the type of guy who flaunts it. Sure, he wears designer clothes and designer shoes, and his haircuts are off-the-hook or whatever, but so what? He likes to look nice. There's no shame in that.

But Sam was watching me while Creed burned through his flyer with her laser-focused stare in the middle of Sam's book which Charlie looked at without seeing anything. I'm not stupid. I don't think Sam likes me, but that doesn't mean he won't try to get with me at his party. And that's so not what I'm after. "Your brother doesn't like parties," I tell her. "They're really not his scene, and Sam said if Charlie doesn't go, we don't go."

Creed pouts. I know she's trying to be cute but it's kind of annoying. "Why can't you let me have this moment of celebration? Quit being such a downer. I've *just* been invited to my first high school party, and it's not just any party. It's *Sam Birk's* party. Did you know he puts a limit on how many people he invites?" She waves it in my face. "I'm telling you, he could sell these flyers like tickets."

I resist the urge to roll my eyes. "Okay. I get it. It's a big deal." I peek at the stalls for any shoes. "You need to keep your voice down. He told you to keep it on the down low. This is not the down low."

She breaks eye contact. Her eyes go straight to her phone. She's hiding something. "Did you tell people you were invited?" I ask.

"Just a few of my haters," she says as she drags a foot across the floor.

"What if he uninvites you," I say.

She blinks a few times, folds the invite in half and then another half before shoving it in her back pocket. "He wouldn't do that."

I turn to look in the mirror. I wash my hands for something to do. "You don't know that. He might."

She shrugs. "He's Charlie's best friend. You need to chill out. I won't tell anyone else. It'll be fine." She gives me a playful shove. "You and Charlie would totally make a cute couple," she teases but I see the worry in her eyes. "You're both a little too OCD to have any *real fun.*"

I hate how much I love the thought of us being a couple. "Yeah, right," I tell her as we walk out. "I would never date your brother. He's totally not my type," I continue as we head to our next class. I'm totally talking out my butt and it's so stupid. Why am I saying things about Charlie that I don't even mean just to make his extremely immature sister happy? Oh, yeah. Because we're best friends. Because she's the first girl who was like halfway nice to me since the day I moved here. That's why. And in spite of the fact I have a huge crush on her big brother and she's kind of hard to take at times, especially when she drools over the biggest boy slut at Seeberger High, she's really funny, smart, sweet, and real.

So I guess I shouldn't hold it against her that she likes a guy who has slept with half the female population that walk these hallways. I mean, I like a guy who doesn't acknowledge the existence of ninety-five percent of the student body because he's too busy dreaming about an unknown species of clown fish that may or may not exist. Creed jokes about her brother and I being a couple, but I doubt she'd be this chill if she found out I seriously like him.

My phone vibrates just as we step into the hall. I turn away from her to look at the screen. It's Sam. I shove the phone in my pocket and keep walking. My level of anxiety is rising. He's so irritating. Why is he Snapping me? He has to know how she feels about him. I rush out of school toward the parking lot. I'm almost to my car when someone walks up beside me. "Hey, Venus," Sam's telltale deep voice is in my ear.

"What?" I ask.

"I texted you," he says with expectation in his voice.

"Oh, did you," I reply, as if he's the most boring, unimportant person in the world and not the school calendar boy. I climb into my Forester and try to shut the door.

His hands hang over the top of my door, as he leans on it. I hate how the sun hits him just right in the face, lighting up his eyes that are already perfect, even though I do not like him. Well, mostly don't like him. An insecure look of self-doubt crosses his beautiful face. Why does this thrill me? I never thought of myself as a mean person. *Focus, Venus. Stop staring at the partial Greek god.* If Creed catches him standing by my car she's going to hate me. "Get in the car," I order.

"Okay?"

Sam is barely in the car and I'm practically peeling out to get somewhere else. Dust flies everywhere. His door slams. "Slow down, woman. Damn."

I barely miss the huge pothole as I fly out onto the road. "What do you want?" I demand.

"Didn't you read my text?"

"I've already said that I didn't," I all but roar. I feel a little out of control, and I wish I didn't like it so much. Sam sits there like a mute idiot in the passenger seat. "What did it say?" I ask.

"I asked if you were coming to my party," he says, while he stares straight ahead. I see Charlie about the time he sees me. We pass by each other in slow motion, even though I'm pretty sure I'm driving fifteen miles over the speed limit. I tap my brakes. The last thing I need is a speeding ticket in a residential area. Charlie's look of surprise is stuck in my brain. I feel like the worst sort of traitor.

"Well," I say. "That's just great."

"What?"

"Did you not just see your best friend see us together?" I demand as I wave wildly at the front windshield.

"Yeah, so?"

I slap my steering wheel. "The only thing that would make it worse is if she was with him," I mutter.

"What are you talking about?" he asks.

I swear. Guys are so dense. I slam on the brakes. "You can get out now," I tell him as I park on the side of the road.

"This isn't anyone's house," he argues.

"Your car is back at the school, so go find it," I demand. I feel like the world's biggest bitch, but I tell myself I don't care. It's his fault I'm dumping him on the side of the road.

"Yeah. I know," he says. "I've got practice in like five minutes. Coach doesn't like it when I'm late."

I can't believe what I'm about to do, but my hand is on his arm, shoving him against the door. "I guess you better start running," I say as he bumps into the door.

"You really gonna make me walk back," he says, but he's not angry so much as thoroughly confused.

"I didn't ask you to follow me to my car," I say. "Don't do it again." I feel like a crazy person, but Creed would be so crushed if she knew any of this was happening, which is why there's no need to tell her I got a Snap from slutty Sam asking me if I'm going to his party.

He climbs out in super slo-mo which tells me he's not that worried about the coach getting mad at him. "Answer my text," he says before shutting the door and taking off at a slow jog down the street. He runs backward, waving at me in my rearview mirror and wearing the goofiest grin I've ever seen. There's no way the guy doesn't know how gorgeous he is, which is the only reason I don't feel bad for completely ignoring him as I pull out onto the road. I smile bigger as he grows smaller in my mirror.

I'm not about to answer his text just because he told me to. At least not right now. But if I don't answer and he changes his mind about inviting us because I ghost him, and Creed finds out, that won't be good. But if I answer Sam and she finds out I'm messaging him and thinks I'm chasing him, that won't be good either. This is all so stupid.

I'm barely in my driveway and someone is on my bumper. My heart skips a beat when I see Charlie rushing me in my side mirror. I open my door and step out. "What was he doing in your car," he says. He sounds like he's in pain.

"I didn't—" I start to defend myself and then stop. "It's a free country, Charlie," I say as I turn away from him to grab my backpack. I walk through my gate and up the steps that lead to my back door. He follows.

"I am well aware we live in a democracy," he concedes, and I can't help but smile at his matter-of-fact way of speaking. "That doesn't tell me why he was in your car."

I open my fridge to grab my favorite after school treat, a giant chocolate-covered strawberry. Mom makes me seven every week, one for every day. I can't believe I'm about to part with my most favorite food in the world. I offer him the tray. "Would you like one?" I ask.

Charlie eyes them warily. "I don't know. I've never had one."

I shrug as relief passes through me. I'm very serious about my strawberries. I take one and lean over my plate as I take a delicious bite, knowing the juice is going to run, and it does. Charlie's thumb drags over my chin before finding its way to his mouth. Whoa. That's the hottest thing I've ever seen. Why am I not disgusted that he just tasted my juice?

"It's okay," he says before smacking his lips together a few more times.

I force myself to look somewhere else before taking another bite. "It would probably taste better out of the box," I murmur, because I don't know what to say.

He gives me a small grin. "I'll take your word for it. I'd hate to take any of your joy. I can see you like them."

My strawberry is almost gone. I take a smaller bite. "I really do."

"Where is he?" he asks as if he just realized Sam is no longer in my car.

"I kicked him out," I tell him as I stick a bag of microwave popcorn in the microwave.

He studies me even more. "Why?" he asks as I walk into my living room, plop down on the couch, and turn on the television. He stands in the middle of the room, looking lost.

I point to the couch. "Sit down," I say as I turn on my latest addiction – Brooklyn Nine-Nine, a goofy sitcom about a bunch of cops who don't seem to take their job too seriously but it's funny.

He sits awkwardly beside me. The bowl of popcorn is between us. "Have some popcorn," I tell him.

"No thank you. If I eat the popcorn, I'll be thirsty."

I point at my oversized water bottle. "You can have some of my water," I offer, "if you can get over your fear of other people's spit."

His eyes bore into the side of my face. I have no idea what he's thinking, but I can feel that he is. Every ounce of me wants to ask what, but I keep my mouth shut as I try to focus on the mouthy detective on-screen struggle with his not-so-obvious crush on his coworker who is dating someone else. "Has anyone else drank out of it?" he asks.

I shouldn't be so mean, but I can't help it. "Like your sister," I tease.

His nose wrinkles. "Gross," he says as his eyes travel around the room, and I try to see everything from his point of view. My mother and I are well traveled. We have learned to live minimally. She is a big believer in souvenirs and flea markets, which is why we have a bookend shaped like an alligator head with its mouth wide open sitting atop a small round table covered with bright yellow fuzzy flowers that look like someone was on a psychedelic trip when they painted them. Mom says they're the Oregon Grape, or at least that's what the man at the flea market we hit on the way out of town told her. Mom said the alligator head is the perfect contrast to the delicate essence of the flowers. All I know is its quite grotesque. Sometimes I run my fingers over the top of its offensive snout, as if I'm daring it to bite me. It's quite thrilling.

His eyes pause about the same time I remember the pillow I lay my head on. "Is that a naked person?" he asks.

I snatch the throw pillow from behind my head and hit him in the face with the streaker. "Mom bought him in Pasco County Florida," I tell him. "Some old lady embroidered pillows for the nudist colony we drove through. Mom just had to stop and get a souvenir," I tell him with a giggle. "I stayed in the car."

He coughs and averts his eyes. "How old were you?"

I turn up the television. "Twelve."

He glances at the pillow again. "Your mother bought that pillow when you were twelve," he confirms. "Did she let you see it?"

I snort a little at his question. "Who do you think held onto it as she drove away?" I get stuck on my own question. "Wait a minute. How did you get here if you don't have a license?"

His cheeks turn pink. It's so hot. "I drove here because I needed to talk to you," he says like an afterthought. I feel like my heart is singing. I should not be so happy that he's breaking the law for me. "Why would she—why would she buy that?"

I grab it up once more and put it back behind my head. "I guess she liked it," I reason. "Anyway, she said he was the only guy she'd lie beside every night."

"That's weird," he says as he glances at his watch. "I'm supposed to be at the school."

"Why?"

"I volunteered to help clean up the football field."

"Oh, crap," I say. "I'm supposed to be there too. With Creed." My stomach tightens. "She's not going to be happy with me."

He takes the bowl of popcorn and sets it on the floor. His fingers thread themselves through mine. "I do not like this show, but you make it tolerable," he states.

I scooch over so we line up better. I lean my head on his shoulder. "I don't like people talking when I'm watching a show, but you make it less annoying."

He blinks in the corner of my eye. I feel his eyes on me. "Is it terrible we do not care we are not fulfilling our obligations?"

I bump my head on the side of his shoulder before turning just enough to meet his gaze. "I *care*, Charlie. Just not about that." I can't believe how cheesy and honest I'm being, but there's something about Charlie Barren that feels like a safe space. I feel like I could tell him anything. That might be a problem.

FIFTEEN

Charlie

I can't believe I'm sitting in Venus's house, holding her hand, and watching television with her; or rather she's watching television and I'm watching her. I should look away. It's weird that I don't, but I can't. I haven't been able to focus on anything since I saw Sam riding with her in her car. I have never wanted to stab someone so much as I wanted to stab him. I hate how jealousy makes me feel. Like I'm crazy. Because I would never do anything to hurt Sam. Not for real. "Why was he in your car," I say, even though I know I'll regret it.

"I didn't want to hurt Creed's feelings," she answers. She sounds irritated. I think. I'm not sure.

"I don't understand," I respond. I almost tell her that she didn't want to hurt my sister's feelings, so she hurt mine. Because, apparently, I don't have any feelings.

"He followed me to my car, okay? I didn't ask him to. I didn't invite him to. I didn't do anything to make him think I was interested or whatever," she explains. "I know how Creed feels about him, and I didn't want her to see him at my car, so I told him to get in. I just had to get out of there," she says as she waves her hands around. "And then I saw you driving down the street, so my plan backfired. I guess I'm just stupid. I don't know."

Her words confuse me even more. "I never said you were stupid."

Her arms are folded. She's chewing on her lip. Her eyes are watery like Creed when we fight. I think she's getting angry.

"You didn't have to," she whispers.

"Why would I?" I reply because never in a million years would I call her stupid. I don't know why she would say that.

"You don't have to say it because it is implied," she blurts before hopping off the couch and running into the other room. Her loud voice startles me, and I flinch at the same time she jumps up.

I stare at the television. I'm pretty sure I should say something, but I don't know what. I know I should stop asking questions because they upset her, but there's something I still want to know. My head aches from trying to sort it all out. "Why was he at your car," I yell into the empty space of her living room.

"He asked me if I was going to his party," she says from somewhere behind my head. Her warm breath just went down the back of my neck. My face heats along with every other part of me. I grab her naked man pillow and hold it against my stomach, mostly ignoring the picture as I squeeze it.

"You know he'll just keep asking until you say yes," I tell her even though I don't want to. I wish I knew what she was thinking about this stupid party.

"I didn't tell him I was going," she says before holding something out. "Want some Nutella? This chocolate is as sticky as poo, but I love the little sticks. They are so adorable."

I take it from her hand, being careful not to touch her. "Thank you," I say as I peel the paper lid back. "I've never tried Nutella or poo," I answer.

"Well. That's a relief."

"So I see you are a true crime fan," I say, as I study the disturbing number of DVDs with horrible titles that make me glad I can't see their covers.

"Um, no. Actually, I am not. That's my mom. She loves real detective shows." She shoves her feet beneath her butt. "I think they reassure her it's perfectly normal to have life 360 on my phone, a tracker on the underside of my car, and security cameras on every corner of our house." She points at the creepy painting hanging on the wall with an eye in the middle. "Mom isn't really into the third eye thing. There's a camera in the middle of that painting. That's an actual lens watching us right now." She waves. "Hi, Mom," she calls before turning to kiss me.

I'm so stunned all I can do is clutch my plastic container of chocolate poop with one hand and a naked man on a pillow with the other.

"We're making out on the couch," she sings before releasing her hold on me to grab a miniature thing that looks like a breadstick and dip it in the chocolate.

I shove the pillow away from me. "You taste like chocolate," I tell her. That was one of the strangest moments of my life, and apparently, I'm on camera, but I can't stop smiling.

"Shut up, Charlie, and eat your chocolate," she tells me, and so I do. She lets out a long, dramatic sigh. "Since you're not going to stop talking and interrupting my Nine-Nine, we may as well watch something you like."

Venus flips through the channels until she lands on National Geographic. I sit in happy silence as we watch baby animals in the wild. This lasts for as long as it takes for the two of us to dig chocolate poo from every corner of the tiny plastic container. Venus has no sense of propriety when it comes to chasing chocolate, but I guess I don't either. I want to ask her about the kiss, but that would be weird. Wouldn't it?

Her toes sneak closer and closer to my thigh, making me feel like the spider on the screen with its tiny hairs picking up vibrations on its nightly hunt. I wonder if I would feel this way about any girl sitting beside me on a couch, or if it's just Venus. I don't know. I've never sat beside a girl before who wasn't my sister. I wish I could shut off all of my weirdness. "What are you thinking about?" she asks just as the Goliath tarantula digs its fangs into the squealing field mouse with such ferocity I have to look away.

"Spider hairs," I say as I point awkwardly at the screen.

She wrinkles her cute little nose. "Gross," she says as she unfolds her legs to walk into the other room. Her hand is out. "Give me your trash."

I stand up. "I have legs," I say, while feeling like my mom. She loves to say that. All the time, especially to Creed, who loves to act like she is helpless around Mom. Mom calls it the *baby syndrome* because Creed is the youngest. I don't call it anything because I'm usually walking away from whatever request Creed makes of Mom, who usually grants it, because Mom doesn't mind being a servant.

"C'mon then." Venus beckons. And I follow.

The kitchen is relatively small. It is very colorful. "Every wall is a different primary color. Royal blue, golden yellow, and rad red," Venus says as she spins in a tiny circle in the middle of the room. "Except for this guy," Venus stops twirling. She points to the small wall space above the sink. "John Deere green is our one secondary color, or as I like to refer to him, Dear John," she says before turning back to smirk at me. "I like to recite Dear John letters while I wash dishes," she continues with a shrug of her shoulders. "It passes the time."

"Dear John letters," I repeat.

She raises one eyebrow. "Don't tell me you don't know what a Dear John letter is, the famous *it's not you, it's me* letter between two star-crossed lovers whose good luck has just to come an end," she says as she lifts her head to stare at something on the ceiling behind my left shoulder. "Lame attempts to let someone down as easy as possible while telling them they just don't do it for you, that you're not meant to be, and that they are no longer your harbor in the storm," she says while extending one hand out in front of her. The back of her other hand rests against her forehead. "Words of a woman who has lost her love for her man," she declares in a weird, breathy voice.

"Oh. Okay," I say.

She straightens up and flashes me a grin before doing a half bow. "State forensics champ two years running. Thank you. Thank you very much," she declares as she pops back up, salutes me, and gives me a wink. "And that's all you get, sailor." Her eyes sparkle and shine. I want to stay in this moment where her face fills every part of my brain until there is nothing left to think of but her and how perfect her every imperfection is to me.

I think I hear a buzzing, but I'm not sure. All I see or hear is Venus. She steps closer. She stops moving when her toes bump my shoes. She drops her arm to my side, but she gazes into my eyes. I gaze right back. Her elbow brushes the front of me as she holds her cellphone in front of her face. Her eyes are glued to her phone right before she shrieks and jumps around in circles. "He gave her a ride home from school," she sings. "Oh, this is so, so, sweet." She gives me a shove. "Go! Get out of here. Your sister's going to wonder where you've been."

I stumble and trip down her steps outside. "Who gave who a ride?" I ask.

"Sam gave Creed a ride home," she says before the door shuts, and I'm standing all alone.

"Oh, shit," I say as I jog to the car. "I've got to get to work on that list."

SIXTEEN

Venus

I can't believe Charlie followed me home, just like I can't believe how normal it felt sitting beside him on my couch eating Nutella. I amble back to the living room, plop down in the couch, and lean over to snatch up the bowl of popcorn before resuming Brooklyn Nine-Nine. Andy Samberg and his obnoxious mouthy self make a wonderful Rookie cop. He makes me giggle. He's so funny. And quirky. Just like every other person on the show. "Just like Charlie," I mouth and eat some more popcorn while I wonder if Mom has a camera behind the painting on the wall or not. I honestly don't know, but the wondering keeps me guessing, and the guessing makes my nerves jangle. I like a little anxiety. It's kind of fun.

I stare down at my phone. I wish I could tell Creed about my ginormous crush on her brother, and that I've kissed him a few times, and each time was total devastation, but in a good way. Like what I imagine cutting into a molten lava cake will be someday when I get to eat one. All squishy, sweet, and warm. And then the magical moment will happen, the hot chocolate will spill out into a perfect puddle of delicious goo. One bite will take me to my knees, just like Charlie's kiss.

"Dang it," I say to no one. "I guess we're going to Sam Birk's party."

I pick up my phone and Snap Sam. "Since I have nothing better to do, I might make an appearance." I hit Send.

"Cool, cool," he says before sending me a picture of Creed's backpack on the floor of his car. "Gave your friend a ride home today. Who says I'm not charitable?"

My jaw drops. He's such a jerk. Why does he have to be so clever and cute? "You're kind of full of yourself," I reply.

"Ouch. Hurtful. I'll forgive you for that one since you're smokin' hot." Emoji flame.

I read his message twice. I hate that it makes me excited. "I will not respond in kind," I tell myself as I try to think of something unflirty to say back. I don't want to sound too judgy, because then he'll think I'm a choir girl. Which I'm not. I'm just particular. And not stupid. Starting something with Charlie's best friend and my best friend's crush would be the worst decision I've ever made. Sam is hot, but he's not worth losing Creed.

I hold my phone over the alligator's mouth and Snap a pic. I put a bunch of sleeping emoji's in my message. "Bored. Later gator." I type before I hit Send.

"OMG," Creed's message reads. Like ten times over. "I still can't believe Sam gave me a ride home. Should I text him?"

My stomach hurts. "How many times have you already texted him?" I ask.

"IDK. Like five or six times. But some of them were GIFs and one was a TikTok link."

I'm so panicking inside, So I Facetime her. "Hey," I begin, trying to sound all chill.

"What's up?" she replies from where she lays on her stomach. "I rode in Sam Birk's car."

I resist the urge to roll my eyes. "I know," I say. "And I am sure it was very exciting," I continue in the most patient manner I can manage, as if I'm talking to a four-year-old. "But you have to chill out," I continue.

"He's so hot. I wonder if he'll take me to school tomorrow," she gushes.

This has to stop. Now. "Creed," I yell into the phone like a madwoman.

"What," she says. Her blue eyes are all soft and dreamy. I hate popping her Sam-induced bubble, and the only thing I hate more than that at this exact moment is Sam Birk, who I am pretty sure is blowing up my phone. "You seriously have to not text him any more today. At all. Do not text him until he texts you. If you smother him, he will run away," I explain.

"Oh," she says. She sounds so deflated. I am so mean. But me hurting her feelings is so much better than Sam crushing her soul, which he will inevitably do sooner than later if she doesn't stop. "The key to guys like Sam is completely ignoring them," I tell her. "Don't make it so easy for him to have access to you," I continue while acting like some sort of brilliant teenage love guru when really I have no clue. But it sounds good. Channeling unapologetic Gina who shoots from the hip off Brooklyn Nine-Nine is as fun as I thought it would be. "He will chase what he thinks he cannot have."

"Really?" she asks.

"Really. I know it goes against every fiber of your thirsty being, but you have to pretend Sam Birk doesn't exist."

Her lips form a pout. "What about at home? Can I still daydream about him?"

"Yes. Just don't *tell* him."

"So I have to pretend that my crush doesn't exist. I can't look at him. I can't smile at him. I can't talk to him at school," she drones on.

"I know it sounds crazy, but I'm telling you. If you can do all that, by the time we go to his party, your indifference will drive him crazy," I assure her.

"It's going to be very hard, but I'll try," she whines. "What about all the things I've already sent him. What do I do about that?"

I hope my face doesn't show how cringey I feel at the thought of what she may have sent him. "Has he responded to any of them?" I ask.

"Well, no. But I kind of sent a lot in a short amount of time, and he's probably on his Xbox."

I peek at my messages. They're all from Sam. "Seriously," I say as I scan them.

"What? He likes Xbox," she says in a defensive tone.

"Oh, yeah. I bet you're right," I say as I focus on her.

"Hey, where'd you go?"

"I was looking at something."

"Who texted you? Was it Charlie?"

"It was my mom," I lie. There's no way I'm telling her Sam is Snapping me which is why he's not Snapping her. And I would yell at him about it, but I don't want to give him the satisfaction of telling him we're talking about him. "I better go. I've got a few chores to do," I say. *Like telling Sam Birk to quit being an idiotic thirsty boy. I'm going to his stupid party. What more does the guy want from me?*

"I gotchu. Totes. Charlie wouldn't text you anyway. He doesn't like text anyone. Ever." She rolls her eyes. "I swear my brother doesn't know what to do with his phone other than use it like an Encyclopedia." She gives me a wave. "Byeeee."

I point at the screen. "Remember. Sam Birk does not exist. Ignore him. Do not text him. Do not stalk him online. Do not Like his social media posts."

"Yes, Mother," she grumps before ending the call.

I open up my phone to Sam's barrage of messages that are a pictorial story of a girl passing a boy on the street without noticing him. His eyes bug. His hand goes to his heart. His head drops back. His knees bend just enough to suggest he's on the way to the ground. She doesn't look back. The last clip is a lightning striking a heart before it shatters. I can't help but smile. Sam is way too smart for his own good. I hate how much I want to save it, or that every time I see him, I'm going to remember this adorable story.

"So I'm in a film club at school," Sam says.

"Oh?"

"What'd you think?"

If you were my crush, it would be the most perfect thing I could ever receive. Yeah, definitely not saying that. "It's alright," I type but then delete it. I'm not that cruel. It's a masterpiece. "What's the title?" I ask.

"I haven't gotten that far yet," he replies.

"Tell me when you do," I answer.

"What do you suggest?"

"It's not my work," I fire back. I'm starting to get annoyed because all I can think of is Creed waiting to hear back from him and he's talking to me.

"But you're my muse," he says.

Ugh. Now I'm definitely annoyed. "I didn't ask to be," I say.

"Venus Rising," he says.

I say nothing.

"Venus Strikes Again," he Snaps.

I giggle and hate myself for it.

"The Victory Trail of Venus," he Snaps.

"Please stop," I say out loud.

"Venus Ripped My Heart Out," he Snaps.

"I did not," I reply. "Please stop Snapping me," I say.

Silence is what I get. I can't believe how much it bugs me, even though it's what I said I wanted. I lay the phone down and go look for chores to do. I may be talking to my best friend's crush more than I should, but at least I'm not a liar.

SEVENTEEN

Charlie

Mom made my favorite meal, which makes what I'm about to do even harder, but I'm desperate. "So Sam and I had a fight," I say as I pass the mashed potatoes to Dad.

"About what?" Creed demands. She stares me down.

Crap balls. Why didn't I think this through? "I saw him riding with a girl I like," I say.

Mom's face lights up like a lightbulb from the other end of the table. "You like a girl," she says. I can tell she doesn't believe me. This is not going at all like I want it to.

"What girl," Creed shrieks in my ear. Her hand wraps around her fork. I move farther away from her.

"Keersten," I blurt, because it's the first name that comes to my mind. I can't believe it's only been two weeks since I met Venus. Can a person fall in love in two weeks? Am I in love? Does thinking about a girl every waking moment constitute love? Does wondering what she looks like when she rolls out of bed in the morning mean more than just a crush? Does knowing what she's eaten for lunch every day since she's been a student at Seeberger High make me a stalker or just very observant? My food sits in my stomach like a weight. I wish I could ask Sam these questions, but I can't. He'd probably call me a freak, or worse, slap me on the shoulder and give me some words of encouragement that he

127

doesn't mean because I'm too weird for any girl to really like me. A few kisses doesn't mean anything. Or does it? Why would she kiss me if she wasn't interested? Or did she kiss me to see if I'm a good kisser, and she obviously doesn't think I am or she would keep kissing me? Right? I think I'm getting a headache.

"But that's over with," Creed argues. Her words pull me out of my head. Her eyes water. She looks like she's going to cry. I'm a terrible brother because I'm relieved to be pulled out of my agony over wondering if her best friend likes likes me, or just likes me. Like when she texts me, are we talking or just texting?

"Charlie," Creed's sharp tone interrupts my pondering over the significance of what may or may not be between me and Venus.

"What."

Her eyes narrow. "I said I didn't know you like *Keersten*." She sounds like she doesn't believe me.

"Yeah, so," I answer, echoing Creed's usual defiant tone. She stares at me like a bug under a microscope.

"I still don't believe you," she says after the longest time.

The big bite of mashed potatoes sticks to the back of my throat, threatening to choke me. Or maybe it's her certainty as she calls me on my lie. Somehow, I get them down. I take a big drink of lemonade. "Well, you don't know everything."

"Who's Keersten?" Mom asks.

"The biggest ho on the cheer team," Creed answers, but she doesn't turn away from staring at me.

"Creed. That is a very unkind thing to say," Mom scolds.

"Well, it's true," she argues.

I recall what I set out to do. "Yeah, she kind of is," I agree. "Which is why Sam likes her so much," I continue.

Dad spits a little lemonade on his plate.

"Well," Mom repeats. "I'm sure there are other reasons your *best friend* likes her. Sam is such a sweet boy," she scolds. "I'm sure he wouldn't do anything to hurt you on purpose, Charlie. Maybe he doesn't know how you feel about her, or maybe her car broke down."

"Mom," Creed practically wails. "This isn't the fifties. Her car didn't break down. If Sam gave her a ride anywhere, it's only for one reason," she cries before tossing her napkin down beside her plate. "May I please be excused?"

Dad swats the air. "Go ahead, honey. You're excused."

Creed stomps away from the table. Mom and Dad stare at me. It's hard to enjoy my food when it feels hard and dry going down, but I'm still hungry. I reach across the table and grab the roll off Creed's plate. "So as I was saying, I'm mad at Sam for driving around with the girl I like, because he *does* know how I feel about her."

I steal glances at Mom. It's hard to look her in the eye when I'm making all this up as I go along, but I have to stick to my plan. I really don't want to go to stupid Sam's stupid party. It's going to be a disaster. He's going to talk Venus into going into his bedroom. I just know it. I butter what's left of my roll crumpled in my fisted hand. "And, you should know Sam gave Creed a ride home today, and I don't think he should be doing that. She kind of likes him," I say before taking a bite of my favorite rolls that Mom makes.

"Is that so?" Dad asks before forking a bean and cramming it in his mouth so hard the metal of the fork hits his teeth, making a terrible sound.

"Yes," I clear my throat. "I just think that Sam and I need to take a break from each other. I don't want him chasing my little sister," I say before scooping up another bite of potatoes. "Which is why we can't to go to his party," I add.

Mom's eyes widen. "You were invited to his party," she says. She looks so excited if I didn't know better, I'd think she was invited to his stupid party.

"Yeah, but I'm not going." I hate the look of disappointment on her face.

"Don't be too hasty, Charlie. It might not be what you think. Sam might really like Keersten. You don't know," Mom says as her cheeks turn pink. "And I'm sure he brought Creed home because he's your friend, and she's your little sister."

"Why didn't you bring her home?" Dad asks.

"Yeah, Charlie. Where were you?" Mom echoes. My stomach tightens. There's no way I'm telling them where I was. Sitting on a couch with the most beautiful girl at our high school who just happens to be my sister's best friend, eating chocolate poo and letting her kiss me on the lips. It was all so wonderful. I can't believe this backfired on me so fast.

"You like Sam more than you like me," I accuse, even though I know it's a crazy accusation and completely untrue. I don't know what else to say to change the subject.

"Char-lie," Mom's voice sounds all tight. A tear rolls down her cheek. I'm the worst son there ever was. "You know that's not true. Your dad and I both love you. So much. We're so proud of you."

Dad's hand covers mine. It's all too much. If I'm not careful, I'll start crying. All I wanted is for them to hate Sam until the party's over and done with. Is that too much to ask? I jump up from my chair. "Praying mantises are cannibals. They eat their young," I protest. "I can't believe you'd believe in Sam more than me. I feel like a praying mantis right now. I know what I saw," I insist before stomping out of the room. My head spins. I've gone completely insane, except I'm not. I caught Sam chasing Venus. I'm pretty sure he knows how I feel about her. If he does, why is he doing this to me? I thought *we* were friends.

I want to ask Sam how he feels about her, but I won't. My fists clench at my sides. He knows I would never ask him about her or any other girl. And that makes it even easier for him to try to talk to her. This is so stupid. I hold my phone in front of my face and take a picture. "Please don't talk to Sam. You know he talks to lots of girls," I text on it before sending it to Venus. *I am so stupid*.

"Nice picture of your face," Venus replies. "It's almost as scary as the alligator."

Her words make me laugh, which feels so much better than rage. "Thank you," I answer before laying my phone down. I put on my noise-cancelling headphones and get out my sketch pad to work on the operculum of a Domino clown fish, but somehow the curve morphs into Venus's perfect chin, and the head of the fish becomes the rest of Venus's face. I get lost in two big green eyes on the side of my fish. I dig around until I find the brown and yellow pencils. It isn't long and flowing hair surrounds my Venus fish that floats in still waters while it stares up at me from its page in my sketchbook. I should erase it, but I cannot erase colored pencil marks. I should rip it out and throw it away, but I can't.

I've never drawn anything so ridiculous, and I've spent hours drawing Xenoturbella monstrosa, a purplish gray species of shapeless worm discovered in the deepest canyons of the ocean. They are so simple and basic the only thing they have are mouths, so I suppose they are bulimic. If they can ingest but not process or excrete, it has to come out somewhere or they'd blow themselves up.

I study my drawing once more – undeniable proof I've officially gone off the deep end. A fish with a girl's face is physically impossible. It defies every law of nature. There is no ecosystem in which it could exist. It cannot be classified. I'm a broken boy who may never be a marine biologist, but I think I just created a new species. *Venus fish* I scrawl across the bottom of the page before closing my sketchbook and stare at the ceiling. I can't believe I thought my plan to make my parents not like Sam, the golden boy, would work.

A shadow falls over my face, startling me. My headphones slap against the side of my head as she releases them. "Dude, what the hell?" Creed snarls.

"What?"

"Why are you trying to get Mom and Dad to not like Sam?" she asks. "Cause I know you don't like Keersten."

I can't believe I'm so transparent. "You don't know that. I could like Keersten," I argue even as I fight the urge to gag at her name.

"And why are you hating on Sam? He's your best friend," she says as she stares me down. I want to climb back into my headphones. "He's your only friend," she adds.

No, he's not. Venus is my friend. I'm pretty sure. We hung out today and it was nice, right up until the moment she kissed me. Our time together felt more real than all the time I've spent with Sam. He can't help that everyone wants to talk to him all the time, or that he kind of has ADHD, or that his eyes automatically track every girl who happens to walk by until the next one does. That's just who he is, but it kind of makes it hard to have a real conversation with him when I feel like he hears only half of what I say.

"Maybe I don't need any friends," I tell her. "Maybe I don't like him chasing my little sister. He's a manwhore," I point out. "You know this."

She rocks back on her heels. "You don't know that."

"You think everyone's making these stories up about the girls he's been with," I challenge. "Get your head out of the sand. Ostrich."

She kicks me in the shin. Hard. My eyes water. "This is about the party. You don't want me to go 'cause you don't want to go. You're just trying to sabotage." Her lip quivers. "Just forget it. I'll go to that party whether you go or not. I'm not letting you ruin my good time," she says before squatting down to look me in the eye. "I thought it would be nice for you and me to go to a party together. Just once. And it's not just any party, it's the biggest party at our high school. It's *invitation only*."

I'm so tired of hearing about this stupid party. It's not that special. Sam's not that special. He's just a guy. So what if he's the fastest, the strongest, and the best-looking guy who looks like he belongs in an Abercrombie & Fitch commercial? At least that's what I heard one para tell the other one in the back of history class when they were supposed to be helping a student with their notes instead of drooling over Sam who sat in the first row airing out his pits in his wife beater and sweats after spending two hours in the weight room. I only know this because he announced it to me before sliding into his chair, lifting an arm, revealing his hairy armpits, and taking a big whiff of his disgusting guy sweat. "Dude. I gotta air out my pits," he said before turning toward the sound of giggling in the back of the room where the two paras stood.

"Oh, I'm so sorry," Sam said before flashing them his signature grin. And that's when I discovered two grownass women (as my sister Creed would call them) were not immune to Sam Birk's charms. They're as natural to him as breathing and flexing, which is what he was doing as he leaned to the side to dig through his backpack. "I can put my hoodie on," he offered.

"That's alright you're fine," Mrs. Peak sputtered. "I mean, it's fine. Your undershirt is fine." She faced the other para, who made bug eyes at her. If I saw them, they were obvs to everyone, as Creed would say. I hate it when she shortens words to the point that they are not real words because it's *fire*, which is just one more misconstrued usage of a four-letter word that is as old as cavemen. Creed and I have had many arguments about her basic vocabulary, at which point she ends up calling me grumpy grandpa. My lack of emotion during said discussions infuriates her to no end and this gives me a great deal of satisfaction, almost as much as telling her she's being pretentious, a word she has yet to look up.

"Okay, cool," Sam told the para with his head down. His telltale smirk was there. I saw it. I've known Sam long enough to know he knows his effect on girls. And women, apparently.

Hands clapping in my face pull me out of my head as well as Creed's blue eyes. They broke the standard genetic code and codon tables staring me down. Creed breaks a lot of things.

"You can't go without a ride," I argue.

"If I go, Venus goes," she counters. "She can give me a ride."

"No, she can't. She's not old enough. It's against the law."

"No one is going to pull us over," she argues.

"You're right because you won't be riding with her. She wouldn't take the risk." I'm pretty sure I'm talking just to be talking. Nothing holds back Venus if she wants to do something.

"So if Venus goes, you still won't go," Creed prompts. *Dang it.* She knows my weak spot.

I shrug and pretend the thought of Venus walking through Sam's party in the middle of a bunch of drunk dudes staring at her doesn't tear me up inside. I've never thought throwing dynamite in a lake to catch fish was humane, but the same idea of chasing guys away from my perfect girl is more appealing than I'm comfortable admitting. What is it about Venus being around other guys that brings out a level of violence I'd rather not feel? I've got to get a handle on my emotions. Jealousy makes me feel so ugly.

"I don't think she'll go," I repeat.

"Why do you say that? Have you been talking to her," she quizzes me. Creed is usually all over the place – like a squirrel on Adderall. I need to distract her until I can figure this out. *Yes. That's exactly what I've been doing.* "She's your best friend, Creed," I say. "Why are you so paranoid?"

"Why are you answering my question with a question," she replies. "That's my move."

Move. Move. Dance move. Her words force an idea in my head. "If I were to agree to go to this party," I tell her, "you're going to have to teach me to dance." *When did I become such a good liar? This is not good. I have no interest in dancing but it's something Creed will absolutely not agree to.*

Her face lights up. This is highly annoying. Everything is backfiring. It would probably be much easier to just go to the stupid party. Creed literally spins around the room. "I'm gonna make you a playlist. It's going to be so epic. You will love it so much, you won't even be irritated about dancing," she sings as she claps her hands. "Sam's party is going to be the bomb," she crows before exiting my bedroom as quickly as she had entered. *I am so dead.*

EIGHTEEN

Venus

How did I get roped into teaching rhythmless Charlie how to fast dance? It probably has something to do with the fact that Creed threw her hands in the air and screamed at the ceiling, so I had no choice but to step in as a buffer. If I didn't know better, I would say Charlie is doing all of this on purpose. No one can be this horrible at dancing, save for the adorable look of total concentration on his face that runs a close second to severe constipation. That much facial torture has to be authentic.

I can't think of anything helpful, but then I remember the dancing scene in one of my favorite cheesy romantic comedies, *Hitch.* And so out of sheer exhaustion and desperation, I bring it up on my phone. "Here. Just watch Will Smith, and do what he does," I advise as I play the video clip. My finger taps the screen. "See there? See the stepping side to side? Just do that."

I steal a glance at Charlie, who watches me, not my phone. His bedroom just got a whole lot smaller. Creed's playlist, which mostly consists of Beyoncé, whose music is top shelf but impossible to dance to for beginners, shrinks into the background. "What about slow dancing," Charlie says, and I swear his voice just dropped a whole octave. Whoa.

"Um, okay," I say, as I shove my phone in my back pocket. Either this boy is way smoother than I thought, or he really knows zilch about dancing. "Slow dancing is super easy," I say as I take his hands and put them at my waist. My hands reach for the back of his neck. He tugs me so close my feet find themselves between his. "So it's just like swaying," I say somewhere near his ear. I can't tell if he hears me or not, but we're totally meshing. I open my mouth to tell him and then shut it once more.

I wonder if he feels the jolt of electricity flowing through him at the touch of my hand. His hands feel like they could burn a hole through my cotton tee, but in a good way. He draws me closer still, and we sway to Beyoncé's *Texas Hold 'Em*. I feel his stare as we move back and forth. He's waiting for me to look up at him. I shouldn't, but my curiosity gets the better of me. I wonder if he'll try to kiss me, and then I don't wonder. His lips are on mine. His arms lock around me, pulling me up on my tiptoes. It's as if he's trying to steal all my oxygen. He's so hot.

"Dude. What the hell? The door's not even closed," Creed yells over the music.

I stumble out of his grasp. Mostly. But it's kind of hard to do when he has a tight grip on the back of my shirt. Creed's hand is on his lower arm. "Let go of my best friend," she says.

This is so weird. Charlie's breathing slowly returns to normal. "I'm not—" his eyes leave my face and stray to his hand glued to the side of my waist. "We were dancing," he pleads. "She was teaching me to dance."

Creed pinches the skin on the back of his wrist before twisting it as if she were winding a clock. His fingers release my tee shirt one by one. His dexterity is amazing. "O-kay," Creed drawls out. "I'm pretty sure learning to slow dance does not include eating someone's face off," she scolds before reaching into her pocket. "Chapstick," she says to me as she shoves it in my face.

"Sure," I tell her before twisting the cap off the ball-shaped item in her hand. I rub it across the front of my lips.

Charlie reaches for it. Creed swats his hand away. "No. You're my brother. I'm not sharing my Chapstick with you, you weirdo."

He studies the Chapstick still in my hand. "But I just kissed her and now she put her mouth on your Chapstick, so..."

Creed's nose wrinkles. My face heats. Although he's not wrong, I can't believe he just said all that out loud. Creed snatches the Chapstick from my hand, rubs it across the carpet, and tosses it in the trashcan. "There. Now no one will use it." She jabs two fingers in each of our directions. "Ima forget what I just saw because I love Beyoncé, and her music is transcendent. It makes people do crazy stuff. But no more lip lock between you two. And we are *all* going to the dance. There will be no more sabotage." She gives Charlie a hard shove. "No more dancing lessons for you, bro. You'll just have to figure it out on your own."

Creed takes me by the hand and leads me out of Charlie's bedroom. I can only imagine what she's going to tell me. I kind of want to go back to dancing with him, and it has nothing to do with his burning lips. I think.

She shuts her bedroom door before leaning against it with her arms crossed. "What the heck, Venus? Do you like my brother?"

How do I answer this without making her really upset? "Against my better judgment, I might," I tell her.

Her blue eyes bug. "Seriously? I finally find an *awesome* best friend, and she falls for my brother," she murmurs as she shoves off the door and starts pacing around the room.

"Can we talk about something else?" I ask. I'm pretty sure she doesn't want to talk about my crush on her brother, I kind of threw it in her face.

"Like what?" she asks.

"Like what you're going to wear to the dance to catch Sam's attention," I tease.

She falls back on her bed and stares up at the ceiling. Her legs dangle. She taps her toes on the floor. "I know he's been Snapping you," she says, and my heart sinks.

"Oh," I say.

"Just like I know he followed you to your car the other day," she continues.

I don't know what to say. "I didn't want to hurt your feelings," I say. "I wasn't chasing him," I offer.

"I know," she says in a defeated tone before sitting up on her elbows to look me in the eye. I kind of wish she would lay back down. It's easier to talk about this when all I can see is her kneecaps from where I sit on the floor. "I guess I should know if he hasn't noticed me by now, he's not going to," she admits.

"You don't know that," I say. "Who knows what makes a guy notice a girl."

She shrugs like it doesn't matter, but her expression is pained. "It's alright. There will be other guys at the party."

"It's still a Sam Birk Party," I offer. "Which means it will be Off...The...Hook."

She rolls her eyes and lays back down. "That saying is like so last year."

I suppose I should be offended, but her snark makes me smile. She's not down for the count yet. "I guess I'm fine with you dating my brother, so long as you don't break his heart," she says.

"That's what Sam told me," I tell her, and her head pops up.

"Seriously?" I hate the hope I see in her eyes.

"Yeah."

"Awww, that's so sweet. He's such a great friend to Charlie." I know she means well, but something about her words twists me up inside. I wonder how many times Charlie has heard those words, or if he believes them. If anything, it's the other way around. Sam is lucky to have a friend like him. Charlie would never chase a girl Sam likes. Not like Sam is chasing me, a fact I very much want to point out to Creed, but don't.

"So, about this killer outfit," I say to distract her.

"Right. I want to wear something that suggests I do not care what anyone thinks about me, that I didn't try too hard to impress, but it also has to recognize the significance of the occasion," she states.

My head hurts already. "Is that all," I answer to her ridiculous request.

"Yeah," she says before staring me down. "Am I missing anything?"

. . .

"No. I don't think so." I pretend to give her question serious consideration.

Nothing other than the fact that this is just a high school party that does not warrant all the worry and stress it is causing you. It's not like a job interview that might determine how you spend the next twenty years of your life between the hours of eight and five.

"No," I repeat more decisively.

"Okay, cool," she replies before diving into her closet. I have a feeling my butt will be numb by the time Creed narrows her choices down to three outfits; none of which will probably be the holy grail that has a pretty good chance of being doused with alcohol seconds from walking through the door if she's lucky. At least that's been my limited experience with attending unsupervised high school parties.

I do my best to stay focused on her mixing and matching and mixing and matching for the next seventy-five minutes. Creed is more than slightly demanding. I can tell she is not impressed by my lack of attention to detail, such as the way her ass looks in the last eight pairs of pants she put on. Those are her words. Not mine. "Which one defines the curve of my butt," she says, and I laugh. Her blue eyes narrow. I think she just took a headshot at me with her eyes.

"Dude," I protest, "You cannot expect me to check out your butt. I don't even know what I'm looking for. Do you look at other girls like you look at yourself?" I honestly want to know. Kind of. I'm not sure.

"No. Of course not. Why would I do that?" She glares at me like I'm the crazy one.

"Because you're asking me to," I explain. "I'm not even going to pretend I know which pair of pants shows off your booty the best," I say. "Besides," I point out. "Do you really want to date some guy who likes staring at your butt?"

She plops down on the bed. "I never thought of that," she admits. She looks like she might cry. I can't believe she's being so moody.

"How about the flowery jacket, the cream-colored shirt, and

the green cords," I say, even though I have no idea what I'm saying.

"You can't wear a denim jacket with cords. That's just too much of everything," she argues before burying her face in her hands. "This is going to be such a disaster," she whines before peeking through her fingers to look at me. "What are you wearing?"

I lean back on my hands. "I suppose whatever I feel like wearing when I get up that day," I offer.

"So like faded blue jeans and a graphic tee," she says.

I look down at my "resting bicycle face" T-shirt that Mom bought me at one of the last women empowerment conferences she attended. "Yeah, probably," I agree.

"Well. I cannot walk into a party with a best friend dressed like a raging feminist, political activist, or hippie tree hugger," she says before returning to her closet. She tosses a solidly colored shirt that's barely a shirt. "Here. Take this. It doesn't fit me since my boobs grew a few cup sizes," she says while planting her hands on her hips and sticking her chest out as if it were necessary.

"O-kay," I say as I secretly decide I'm wearing my favorite pair of black corduroy overalls to cover my belly that's going to be showing if I wear this measly excuse for a shirt.

"And no overalls," she says, as if she can read my mind.

"I'll wear what I like," I say as I drop the shirt in my lap. "You don't get to decide how much of my skin is in the game," I add.

Her blue eyes widen. Her jaw drops. "You're kind of a smart ass."

"Only when provoked," I fire back. I glance at my watch. I can't believe there's only a week before this stupid party that has me tied in knots. I wish Creed would stop making such a big deal about it. I have a feeling it's going to be like one of those things that I get all psyched up for to the point where I give myself hives, and then it's going to be like some big letdown and I'm going to feel like a foolish dope when it's all over.

I steal glances at Creed who stands in front of her mirror holding up shirt after shirt on her front, tilting her head this way and that and wonder what it would feel like to worry that much about what I'm wearing. It makes my head hurt, so I study the decals on my nails before lifting my wrist to sniff the inside of it because it smells like my mom's favorite perfume, and I heard on the radio smelling a pleasant smell sets off something in your brain that helps calm your anxiety and makes you feel better.

"It's a good thing I don't like your brother," I tell her in an ornery voice. "'Cause if I did, I might have to tell you how I love the way he smells like he just took a shower. And I might have to tell you that when he smiles at me in his sneaky little way, it flips my insides. And I might have to tell you that his hands set me on fire."

"A la la la la la," she shouts. "That's enough. That's so gross. He's *my brother.*" But then she gives me a tiny smile. "Buuuttt, it's nice to know someone finds him attractive in the human sort of way."

Her words are so weird. "What other way is there?"

"I don't know. Like maybe on an intellectual level," she says as if it's a bad word.

"What's wrong with stimulating conversation?" I demand. I can't believe how defensive I feel about liking her brother.

Her smile grows. "You really like him," she teases.

I hug myself. "Maybe, but at least I don't like a guy who has worn out the slide on his Tinder account," I joke. Kind of. I have a bad habit of getting testy, and when I get testy I can be kind of mean.

"Back off," she warns. "I'm not the only girl who is half in love with Sam Birk."

"You're right. I'm sure you're not. Take a number and get in line," I grump just about the time I realize what I'm saying.

"It's a good thing you're a clever mean girl," she says, but I can see she's on the verge of tearing up.

"Hey," I say as I take off my white sock and wave it around. "I surrender. I'm sorry. Please don't be mad at me. I just think you guys are too hard on Charlie," I offer.

Her eyebrows shoot up as fast as her blue eyes bug. "Hard on

Charlie?" she blurts, and I wish she wasn't so loud. "My parents are hard on *me*. There's no competing with Charlie. He's so smart. He's such a good student. He's *National Merit Scholar material*," she's practically yelling. What is happening? "I'm just his little sister. Trust me. There's nothing special about me," she says before giving me a sad smile. "Except for the fact that I have a brainiac brother named Charlie who apparently stole my best friend who is now *his* biggest fan."

I am officially the worst best friend in the entire world. "Well," I manage. "Why don't you tell me how you really feel, 'cause I *feel* this is the perfect time to go for ice cream." I clear my throat. "My treat."

She drops her clothes on the floor and claps her hands. "Is that your lameass attempt at an apology," she warns.

"It's the only one you're gonna get and it has a sixty-second timer, so decide already," I reply. "However, Charlie will have to come with."

"Because now he goes wherever we go," she grumps. "No thanks."

"No, because if I drive anywhere with you, I have to have someone eighteen or older in the car," I tell her while trying to hide that I'm kind of dancing inside now that I have a legit excuse for him to go with us.

Her big blue eyes roll in her head. She's a champion eye roller. "Fine, but if he comes, no more making out. Once was bad enough."

I roll my eyes right back at her. "Fine but at least recognize if Sam were here and he was willing, you would totally make out with his hot face right in front of me," I say as I let her pull me off the floor.

She giggles. "I totally would. All. Day. Long." Her face is in mine. This just got weird. "There's only one Sam Birk," she says in a sportscaster voice that sounds like it's about to announce the NFL Draft.

"Thank God for that," I fire right back at her before running out of her room and down the hall to knock on Charlie's door, which he whips open.

His look of utter annoyance changes to the cutest grin I've ever seen in a split second. "Venus."

"Charlie," I reply. Then we just awkwardly stare into each other's eyes until Creed bumps into me from the side.

"Charles, come with us. We need ice cream. Venus is driving and she's buying." She tugs on my arm, yanking me down the stairs. "It's her apology for making me watch you two kiss," she hollers. "Meet us in the car in five. We're starving," she yells in my ear, and I fall against the wall to escape her volume.

I come to an abrupt stop at the bottom of the steps when I spy who I'm guessing are Venus's parents. Her words about our kiss flood my mortified mind. "Mom, Dad. This is Venus. She's my friend," she says before dragging me out the front door.

"Nice to meet you," I get out before the front door slams shut.

NINETEEN

Charlie

I don't know how I feel about my parents knowing I've kissed a girl, but I'm pretty sure I know how they feel as I walk by their beaming faces. This is so strange.

"Mom, Dad. I guess I'm going for ice cream," I say.

"Have a nice time," Mom sings. I can almost imagine the mental jumping jacks going off inside her head. Dad gives me a nod, like what I imagine one of those adult man to adult son nods would go, but I'm not entirely sure. All I know is I've never gotten one. Until now. Who knew kissing a girl was so significant? I know it is to me, but that's for totally different reasons I'd rather keep to myself.

My mind races as I walk toward Venus's car. Now that we've kissed, does that mean Venus will not be checking other guys out at the party, or will she dance with them like she dances with me? Will she lay her hand on their chest over their heartbeat? Will she stand close enough to let her chin touch their chest like she did mine? Will her thumbnail graze the back of their neck in a rhythmic way like she did to me while we were dancing, slowly driving me out of my mind? I've never had anyone mess with my focus like she does, and I wish I didn't like it so much.

Every fish I've drawn on my sketchpad since the first time we kissed somehow morphs into some form of Venus. Her name, her eyes, the decals on her fingernails, or the flowers on her pale pink Converse tennis shoes. I've got Venus on the brain.

While I find kissing her and holding her extremely enjoyable, I do not appreciate her interference with my occipital neurons. It irks me that I cannot draw nature without having her pop up in my head. Repeatedly. The curve in the swan's neck reminds me that her dainty ears are absolute perfection. Green blades of grass match the color of her eyes. Grimy pond water and the way it sticks to my skin feels the same as Venus's touch long after she's away from me, but in a good way.

The horn honks and I jump. Venus waves. "Charlie," Creed yells. "Get in the car."

I walk faster. "Is your seatbelt on?" Venus asks as her eyes meet mine in the mirror.

"Yes," I say as I click it in place. I glance at Creed who makes a bratty face at me in the mirror. "Creed doesn't have her seatbelt on," I tattle.

Creed sighs in an overdramatic fashion before making a big show of putting on her seatbelt. "There. It's on. You happy?"

Venus backs out of our driveway so slowly I can hardly tell we're moving. "I'm thrilled," she answers. "It's reassuring to know if someone rearends me, you won't go flying through the front windshield. I'd hate to see any part of your beautiful face eat glass."

"Wow. You're as literal as Charlie."

"I agree," I say but I'm referring to Venus's statement about my sister hitting her head on the glass. That would be a gruesome sight.

"That wasn't a compliment," Creed grumps at the two of us.

Creed's words and Mom's face come back to me. "Thanks for outing me to Mom and Dad," I mutter.

She whips around in her seat. "It's no big deal," she argues, but I think she feels kind of bad. "Besides, it was an accident."

"You could talk a little quieter you know," Venus adds. "You didn't have to like announce it to the neighbors. You screamed in my ear."

"I wasn't yelling," Creed fires back. "That's how I talk. I didn't know they were going to be downstairs." She leans back in her passenger seat and crosses her arms. "If you don't like me sharing your business, stop kissing my best friend."

Venus giggles. "You walked right into that one," she says, and I can't tell if she's serious or joking.

"I'm not going to stop," I say, because I don't like feeling stupid. And I want to be sure she knows how I feel.

Creed whips around again. "Do you not understand what *awkward* means? She's sitting right here," she says as her hand goes up and down beside Venus. "Seriously."

I stare out the window. "I am aware that Venus heard me. That's why I said it." I don't know why Creed is acting like I'm the one who can't figure things out.

"So were we going for ice cream?" Venus kind of shouts.

"I don't know," Creed answers. Her eyes are all blinky in the rearview mirror. Why is she acting like she's upset?

"Well, you choose," Venus says in a voice that sounds like she's trying to look like a shiny new penny. "Anywhere you want. Within reason."

"How far can we drive?" my sister asks.

"We can't go more than an hour away," Venus offers.

My stomach tightens at her words. This will seriously cut into my prescheduled personal drawing time, but she already has, so I guess it doesn't matter. I was supposed to be drawing the Man of War, the most dangerous jellyfish in Australia. Instead, I ended up sketching Venus's shoe with a bunch of shoelaces dangling from the eyeholes. I can't help but grin at the thought of a jellyfish shaped like her shoe floating around in the ocean, stinging people repeatedly.

"What do you think, Charlie?" Venus's voice interrupts my picturing her pale pink shoe stalking its next victim somewhere off the coast of Sydney.

"Death," I reply.

"Excuse me," Creed answers. "Did you just say death?"

My face heats. I think I answered the question wrong. "What did you ask me?"

"I said, what do you think," Venus says. "About driving an hour to get ice cream."

"Oh. It better be good ice cream," I answer.

We're on the edge of town when we pass the most popular place to eat hamburgers, but I don't know why. Their food is so gross. It always gives me a stomachache.

"Ooh, pull in there," Creed shouts as she grabs the steering wheel. Venus slaps her hand down.

"Do not do that," she orders. "You're going to make me wreck," she says as she keeps a steady rate of speed. "Why do you want to go there?"

"Never mind. This is dumb. We've already gone past it. I just want to go home," Creed pouts.

"I didn't say I wouldn't go back. I just want to know why you want to go there all of a sudden," Venus keeps up her line of questioning despite the fact that Creed is in a full-on pout.

"I just had the urge to eat their fries."

"Their fries are disgusting," I argue. "You know they are because the last time you ate there you spent the next three hours in the bathroom throwing up."

"So I won't eat their fries."

"But you just said you want their fries," Venus argues.

"You guys stop ganging up on me," Creed yells. "Why can't I change my mind about where and what I want to eat? It's a free country."

I look closer at the parking lot. "Sam's car is there. That's why you want to go."

Creed flips me the bird but keeps her silence.

Venus's fingertips tap her steering wheel. "We could go there and watch you agonize over Sam and his ability to completely ignore you or find you a bit stalkerish, or we could go have our own fun while eating delicious ice cream in another town."

I want to agree with Venus. So bad. But I think if I do Creed might shoot her very reasonable, rational idea down. Venus is so smart. I sit on my fingers so I don't give my excitement away by twiddling my thumbs. I look out the window and try not to show any emotion. Creed can be a real pain in the butt when she gets in a mood.

"Fine. I guess we can keep going," she grumps.

"So, Charlie," Venus announces my name like she's standing in the middle of an audience holding a mic. "You know Sam best. What sort of outfit does a girl have to wear to get his attention?"

My stomach turns as hard as a rock. I can't believe she's asking me this after we just kissed, but what I can believe is that she wants him to notice her. "As little as possible," I growl before leaning back in the backseat and staring out the window. I don't want ice cream anymore. I just want to go home. I glance over at Creed. She looks about as happy as I feel. I can't believe Venus is talking about getting Sam's attention to me or Creed, but sadly, I can.

Venus glances at me and then over at Creed before reaching out and turning on the radio. My joy ride just turned into a suck ride. I sink down into the seat so I can't see outside before grabbing up Venus's open notebook. I steal a pen from her door pocket and start drawing one of the ugliest fishes in the ocean, the illuminated netdevil. It is shaped like a round balloon with a beard hanging down below. It has a disgusting little round eye that is all cloudy and looks like it has permanent cataracts, and its teeth look like stalactites, the creepy things that hang from the ceilings of caves. I find myself partially drawing Sam's face on this fish that looks like it swam out of a crypt.

TWENTY

Venus

It's finally the night of the party. It's been a long week. Creed talks to me here and there, but Charlie is giving me the serious deep freeze. He won't look at me. He won't acknowledge me. I've been over to Creed's a few times this week. As soon as Charlie sees me, he leaves the room. I can't believe how much more it hurts than my ex-boyfriend who would get all cold and indifferent when he was in a pout and Charlie's not even my boyfriend. We've kissed a few times, but that doesn't mean anything. Apparently.

I don't know what the heck his problem is, but I'm done dealing with men who act like little babies. I'm going to go to this party tonight and I'm going to have fun. And I'm going to keep an eye on Charlie. And Creed. To make sure she doesn't do anything really stupid like go off into a room with some guy because she's upset because Sam Birk is a total tool.

I know how much tonight means to her, which is the only reason I'm enduring yet another exhausting session of watching her try on every single thing in her closet. An hour later, she has finally decided on her outfit. But now she has to do her makeup. I'm decent at doing makeup, which I tell her, but she insists on finding the perfect YouTube tutorial. That takes another grueling forty-five minutes. Just when I think we're going to go, she deliberates over which shoes to wear for twenty more minutes.

After all this, she looks at me. "Is that what you are wearing?"

I give Creed her own signature bug eyes. "This is what you picked out for me to wear," I tell her in the most emotionless tone I can manage. "I am not changing." I will jump out her second-story window before I step out so much as a shoe.

"Fine," she says. "If you look raggedy, maybe guys will notice me more."

I know she's being all snarky to use reverse psychology on me, but I'm not changing. It's just a friggin' high school party, is the last thing I tell myself before Charlie sticks his head in the door.

His dark hair is styled and gelled. I can smell his cologne from here. A drip of water runs down his neck. He just took a shower, and he smells sooo good. And what is with the stone-washed jeans and lightweight forest green sweater that makes his eyes pop? *Holy buckets, Batman. Charlie Barren smolders.* And he's acting all chill like he doesn't know. He so knows. Why else would his sexy little smirk morph into a sneaky small smile before he walks toward me? His gaze stays on his sister. "Where's your fish shirt, Charles," Creed teases.

His shirt brushes against my arm as he turns his back on me to stare her down. "Mom went shopping for me for Sam's party. I feel a bit like a princess, or should I say prince," he says before turning back around to look at me. "I think I've been royally flushed," he says in a whisper while giving my lips a linger as he walks out.

Whoa. That was like so many dramatic nineties movies I've seen and so hot. I stare at Creed, trying to figure out how much she saw or heard. "My brother is so weird," she says. "I mean, he looks normal. He even looks decent in what he's wearing, but then he opens his awkward mouth."

He doesn't look normal. He looks gorgeous. And his words aren't weird, they're perfection, just like the way he looks at me like he's never thought of another girl. Ever. In his life. The thought of him walking into the party looking like that makes my stomach hurt. He's been transformed. He walked in here acting like it was his bedroom. His usual sketchpad was nowhere to be seen. His glasses he's always wearing that border on nerdy, even though I love them, weren't on his face. "Does Charlie have contacts?" I ask.

Creed gets a blank look on her face. "Um, yeah. I guess so."

"But he didn't before today," I say, even though I know I should shut up because she's going to notice I'm a little too fixated on her brother.

"Nope," she says in a tone that tells me to stop talking about her brother.

And I have every intention to, but I'm not done. "It was weird seeing him without a fish on his shirt or wearing like exercise pants or whatever."

"You mean his athletic pants even though he's never been into sports," she supplies. "He just wears them because they are more comfortable."

"Yeah. I don't think I've seen those jeans on him before."

"Did you not hear what he said," she barks. "Mom bought him brand new clothes just for Sam's party." Creed's lower lip juts out. "Guess she figured I didn't want any new clothes. It's special for me too."

I tilt my head sideways and make a face at her. "Maybe she's waiting for you to clear out some closet space before adding more stuff to it."

She points at her pile of clothes on the bed. "What do you call that? I cleared out some space."

I wrinkle my nose. "I call that a big ole' mess. Are you gonna put 'em all back before we go to Sam's party house?" I hate that I feel all cool talking about Sam's mansion. But it fricking is. He's still sending me flirty Snaps or whatever. Like one day he walked through the whole first floor which took him way longer than it should which tells me his home is crazy huge. Near the end of the video, he yawned really big and adorable, like it was exhausting for him just to walk the bottom floor of his home. Right before he ended it he hugged the kitchen staff and gave her a noisy kiss on the cheek. He has *kitchen staff*. It was after this Snap that I had to answer, and so I did, telling him he was so Extra, and I could not believe he was being so braggy about his wealth by sending me a picture of the help.

He Snapped me right back, telling me she likes to be on camera, and because of him and his Instagram and TikTok fame, she now has so many more followers, and she was super excited to be known as Sam Birk's personal chef.

I laughed out loud. I couldn't help it. He's pretty charming when he wants to be. I texted him back and told him he was full of crap, and that his cook was not stupid. She has to tolerate him because that's her job. And then I immediately felt bad for having so much fun kidding around with him on Snapchat and I stopped responding because I knew Creed would be so sad if she knew. And then I thought about Charlie and how he would not care that I was talking to Sam and then I was sad.

And now the three of us are going to a party at Sam's house because none of us can stay away, because it is Sam Birk. Well, Charlie could stay away, and has managed to, until this year because his sister got invited because of me and so his parents are making him go. So whatever misery Charlie is subjected to tonight falls squarely on my "new girl at Seeberger High" shoulders that are a bit chilled beneath this threadbare shirt Creed insisted I wear. Against her advice, I am wearing my favorite pair of overalls with cotton candy pink Converse to match. I love pink shoes and big pockets.

We jog down the stairs to their front door sounding like a herd of elephants, as my mother would say. Creed barely has a foot out the door when Charlie whooshes by me, knocking his hand against mine. "I call shotgun," he says, and I wait for an atomic bomb to go off. Creed hates riding in the back. She is uncharacteristically quiet. Seconds later she waits by the back car door. That was disappointingly anticlimactic.

I use the key fob to unlock the car doors. I check the rearview mirror and make eye contact with a smiling Creed. "Are you ready for this," I tease.

"I was born ready," she says before sticking out her tongue and making crazy eyes at me.

"Just drive already," Charlie says in a rude manner, catching me off guard. He's a lot of things, but mean isn't one of them.

I back slowly out into the street. "I hope one of you knows how to get there. Otherwise, it might be a long night," I say with my hand on the back of Charlie's seat.

His chin grazes my arm followed by his lips. His movements are so smooth I can hardly believe it, except for my burning ears. I jerk my hand away, hoping Creed didn't see what he just did. My face heats along with the rest of me as I focus on staying on my side of the road. "Stay in your lane, Barren," I joke, except that I'm not. He's so hot.

"Just keep going down this road until I tell you to turn. Then you're going to turn left. Then right. Then left. Then right. Then—"

"Lemme guess, left?" I say. "Do you think I'm that stupid? You're making this up. You sound like a boardgame."

"She's not making it up," Charlie says. "It's a zigzag pattern. That's why we used to call him zigzag Birk. We thought it was hilarious," he says as he turns in his seat to look at Creed. "Remember?"

"Yeah," she answers. "I remember. We thought we were so cool." The wistfulness in her voice makes me feel lonely. "Going to his house was so much fun," she gushes dreamily.

"You used to hang out with Sam Birk?" I ask her. Why didn't she tell me before now?

"Yeah, I did, but then one day my attention hog brother told me I couldn't go there anymore. He didn't want to share his best friend with his lame little sister," she says in a sarcastic tone, but her feelings were hurt. I can tell.

"You were eleven. He tried to kiss you," he mumbles. "That's not cool."

"I didn't mind," she says and crosses her arms.

"Well, I did," Charlie argues. "You're my little sister. I was protecting you."

She sniffs. "Yeah, well. You protected me so well he won't ever look at me again."

"Good," Charlie insists. "The guy's a pig. You know how many girls he's been with. It's embarrassing."

"The only thing embarrassing is your virgin ears, Charlie," Creed practically shrieks before leaning up in between us. "I'm going to that party tonight and if I want to go after Sam, you can't stop me. I'm not a little girl anymore."

"Then stop acting like one," Charlie says drily before putting the palm of his hand on her forehead and giving her a shove. She falls back on the seat. "You messed up my makeup. Now I have to fix it," she grumps.

"Where do I turn?" I ask.

"You missed it about four blocks back," Charlie says in an irritatingly calm manner.

"What," Creed yells, making me jump in my seat. "Why didn't you say something?"

"You're the navigator," he replies. "And I don't care when we get to his stupid party that I don't want to go to anyway. It's going to be super loud, and super annoying, and I'm going to hate every second of it."

I flip a U-ey in the middle of the road and end up half in the ditch that is deeper than I thought. By some miracle, the half of my car that's on the road grabs on the asphalt as I'm peeling out, spitting gravel and rocks from the half that doesn't want to go anywhere. We jerk back up onto the road on all four tires. Creed who's been yelling this whole time, laughs out loud. "Dude. That was awesome."

"You probably took the tread off your tires," Charlie drawls. "You're going to have to replace them before the next winter. Otherwise, you won't have any traction."

"You're such an old woman," Creed scolds, right before I spy red and blue lights in my back window.

"Shit," I say. "Everyone have their seatbelts on?" We all do. I just need to hear them say it.

"Yeah, yeah," Charlie and Creed answer as I pull off as soon as I find a bigger shoulder.

"Lawbreaker," Creed says with a giggle.

"Shut up," I say before rolling down my window to peek out. "Hello, officer," I answer.

He flashes a bright light in my eyes, and then Charlie's before shining it into the backseat.

"License and registration, please," he says, and I hope my registration is in the glovebox as I point at the glovebox, but Charlie just sits there. Unmoving. I bump his knee with the back of my hand as I reach over him to unlock it. Numerous tampons fall into his lap. Creed cracks up all over again. I grab the golden envelope, shine a light on it, and hand it to the officer before flipping my cellphone over to take the license from out of the back attachment.

He shines the light in my face once more. "Have you been drinking tonight, ma'am?"

"Just pop and water," Creed pipes up from the backseat. I wish she would shut up. "I have not drunk any alcohol," I say. "No sir."

"Does she need to walk the yellow line?" Creed asks.

It takes everything I've got not to turn around and yell at her.

"Do *you* need to walk a yellow line," Charlie says to Creed while staring straight ahead. I can't believe this is happening.

The cop looks at me a few more times before taking one more look at my driver's license. He hands it back to me. "Does your mom work at the hospital?" he asks.

"Yes."

"Is she seeing anyone?"

I hope my jaw doesn't drop. "No, sir. She is not," Creed hollers.

He lays a hand on my window and squats just a little. "Tell her Officer Branks says hello. Tell her I gave her daughter a break." He taps on my door. "No more U-turns, missy. And if the evening event you're attending is not shut down by 1:30 a.m., someone's going to be knocking at the door."

I nod but keep my mouth shut. Thankfully so does Creed. He takes his hand off my door. "You all have yourselves a good night and drive safe." He struts back to his patrol car. I ease back out onto the road.

I toss my golden envelope in Charlie's lap, making him flinch. "Yo. Put that back in the glovebox would you, please," I tell him.

"So your mom is the hot new ticket in town," Creed jokes.

It is not funny. I'm way too used to men falling all over my mother, especially when they find out she has a good job. Bunch of lazy, househusband wannabes.

"My mother is a successful businesswoman," I correct her. "What's so wrong with that?"

"Nothing. I'm just saying, if he's asking about your mom's love life, you gotta wonder how many other men are checking her out."

"More like checking her credit score," I grump. "They're only after her money."

"But your father wasn't," Charlie says in a voice that can only be interpreted as affirmative.

"Guess not," I say. "It's just been me and my mom since I was like five years old."

"Wow," Creed says. "That's badass."

I shrug. "Yeah. I guess. I mean she's found a way to spend a good deal of her time at home but still make a living."

"I can't believe we got pulled over by the cops," Creed says in a voice filled with awe. She's so weird. "That is so epic."

"Oh, yeah," I say sarcastically. "So cool. It is my dream to be pulled over for breaking the law."

"It was a U-Turn. What's the big deal," Creed argues.

"She did a U-Turn right before a hill on a double yellow line. The road had no shoulders. The visibility was crap. That's why he should have given her a ticket. We could have been killed," Charlie states as dull and flat as a high school math teacher.

"But we weren't," I argue, even though he has some very valid points. "There was no one coming. I looked both ways more than once." I give him a look. "You're the one who told me I missed my turn. I had to go back."

His arm shoots out in front of me. "Turn left here," he

orders. I stomp on the brakes so I can turn left. "Calm down. You're going to put us in another ditch," he continues.

"I'd let you drive but you can't," I fire back. "*You* calm down. And shut up about my driving already. If you don't like it get your own license to drive."

"Dangg, girl. Someone's feeling feisty," Creed teases from the backseat. I feel like an idiot and a real rip, but seriously. I don't need bookworm Charlie nagging me about my driving when he won't even get a license.

I'm about to ask them both for more directions, but then I see the neon arrow attached to the bottom of the yield sign, so I follow it as I whip a right turn. My tires hit loose gravel, and I'm fishtailing just long enough to make me grip the steering wheel and pray we don't end up on the side of the road as I let my foot off the gas and the brake and wait it out. By some miracle, we stay on the road and my car decides to remember I'm in control. I coast down the gravel until I come to a creep. "What the heck," Creed whines. "Can't you go any faster?"

"I don't want to get dust all over my car," I reason. "Or a flat tire."

Someone whizzes past us, throwing up dust. "Great. I'm driving in a dust storm in the dark," I mutter.

"Turn your brights off. They don't help you see better," Charlie says, but his voice is quiet.

I open my mouth to ask why he knows this fact, but then I stop, and instead flip on my dimmers. "Tonight is so overrated," I grump.

"Tell me about it," he agrees, and I can't help but smile.

"You two are both nerds," Creed announces from the backseat. "You should be glad I love you so much. I'm way too cool for either of you."

"That's debatable," Charlie says and then none of us say anything because we're in awe as we make the last turn. The driveway to the party house is decorated with red lights that run down both sides of the long road that leads to his half-mansion. The trees are filled with white Christmas lights that resemble expensive diamond earrings that dangle from women who walked off the Titanic. It's so over-the-top. I can't help but admire the excessiveness of Sam Birk.

"Do you think he did this himself?" I ask, and then I just feel stupid.

"Of course not. His maid probably did it," Charlie answers.

"Yeah, probably," I answer before looking in the rearview mirror. Creed says nothing. She's too busy gaping at all the lights.

"Check your awe and admiration now, Creed," I tease. "When we get there we're going to be all cool and chill. We go to parties like this all the time," I joke.

She giggles. I pull up behind the two cars in front of me. "You've got to be kidding me," Charlie mumbles. "He even has valet parking." He rolls down the window. "We can park our own car you know. That way we know where to find it."

"If that's what you prefer," the guy says before opening the back door and climbing in. "I still have to go with you to ensure no damage is done to the other vehicles."

If I wasn't nervous before, now I am. Creed opens her door. "I'm not walking in the back door of the house." I watch her walk in front of my car and up the stairs.

"Okay," I say. "Tell me where I'm parking."

TWENTY-ONE

Charlie

I don't know why I said that about the cars. I hope Venus isn't mad at me that I'm making her park her own car, but if I don't know where her car is, I'm going to worry about it the rest of the night. We drive around the back of his house and pull up next to a dark blue Camaro that has red dice hanging from the inside mirror. I feel a little better. I think I can remember a blue Camaro and red dice. The man gets out and jogs off.

Venus clears her throat. "How was my parking job," she says, but I don't think she wants me to answer honestly.

"It was fine," I say.

"Well. That's a relief. I'm so glad I *measure* up to your standards of how I should park *my car*," she barks as she stares out the front windshield. I wish she would look at me. "So are you ready to go inside?"

There are so many things I want to say, so many things I want to tell her. Like please don't fall for Sam. Please don't dance with any guy the way you danced with me. Or why can't we go back to the day before you decided you like Sam instead of me? I overheard Creed talking to her about Sam texting her. I can't believe he would do that to me. Except I can. He's Sam Birk. He can't help himself. He has to hit on any and every girl he might be able to sleep with. The problem with that is its true. He can have any girl. It's always been that way, and it's never bothered me. Until now.

When I think of Sam kissing Venus, it hurts. On so many levels. I hate it.

"Charlie," she says, and I want her to say my name again. And again. And again.

"Yep," I reply as I open my door and climb out of the car.

Venus locks her car twice. "So have you been out here a lot," she says. "To Sam's house."

Her question throws me off guard. We just talked about it in the car, so why is she asking again? "Some when I was younger, but mostly he came to my house since we live in town. It was just easier that way."

I don't think Mom liked driving out here. She never said anything, but I could tell the size of his house that screams "wealth" drove her a little crazy. I don't think it was envy so much as just the idea of living like that seemed foreign to her. Like her conversations with Sam's mother were always kind of stilted. You could tell she never knew quite what to say. Sam's parents are always talking about their trips overseas and places they've stayed, and people they met, and I think my mom just doesn't relate. I don't know. I remember once when I was like eight or nine, I asked Sam's dad how much it cost to boat off the coast of Argentina.

I waited impatiently for him to answer when Mom squeezed my shoulder hard enough I forgot about my question for half a second. "Charlie," she had said with warning in her tone. "We don't ask those sorts of questions." And then she laughed in a way I had never heard her laugh before, a laugh that told me she didn't really think what I said was funny. "I'm sorry, Mr. Birk, but we really must be going. I have something in the oven at home." Mom did not let go of me until we were in the car. "Honestly, Charlie," she had said as we drove away. "I don't know where your mind goes."

My mind was on the water, like it always is. I wanted to know how much it cost to get to Argentina and go out on a boat because Sam's dad had so many beautiful pictures of all the different fish he caught on his trips. I didn't want to catch the fish. I wanted to see them in the water, and I couldn't figure out why my mother didn't know why I asked the question. How was I supposed to know how much money to save up if I didn't ask? My parents had never been to Argentina, but Sam's dad had. I sat on my hands all the way home.

"I didn't know you can't ask people how to get where they have been," I finally blurted as we pulled into our own driveway, because even though my mother was upset with me, I wanted my answer more.

Mom let out a sigh. And then another one. She stared out the window for what felt like forever before turning to look me in the face. "I'm sorry, Charlie. Sometimes I forget that there are questions you have that I cannot answer, but we don't ask people questions about money. It just isn't done." She touched my hand with hers. "Do you understand what I am saying?"

No. I didn't. I'd been around Sam's dad enough to know he never minded talking about his money. He talked about it a lot. But I wasn't about to argue with my mother about it. "Yes, Mom. I understand," I said, because I knew that was what she wanted to hear. I could see in her eyes she was waiting for more, like maybe an apology, but I wasn't about to give her one. I didn't think I had done anything wrong, other than ask Mr. Birk about his money in front of my mother. If there was a next time, I would be sure to pay attention to who was in the room.

After that awkward day, Mom told me Sam could come to our house. And that's how it was until Sam got into sports and I didn't. And then we mostly hung out at school. Mom tried to take me to a few of Sam's games, but it was too weird. I didn't like sitting on the bleachers. They were hard and cold. I didn't like watching Sam run up and down the field. It was boring. And there was something about being with my parents and watching my friend play while I sat between them that felt uncomfortable. Like I felt their unspoken expectations, and it was too much. I don't know if they thought taking me to watch him play sports would rub off on me, or what, but after suffering through his first year of football and hearing my parents argue about attending another one of Sam's games, I had had enough.

When his next season started, I made myself throw up in the driveway on the way to the car. Mom ushered me back into the house. I remember looking back at my dad and seeing the relief in his face once he realized we were not going to go. Creed threw a tiny fit, but she stopped once Dad offered to take her to the mall. And that was the last day we attended Sam's sporting events as a family.

I stare at the back of his house, trying to decide if I should go in the kitchen door or the front door. Venus makes the decision for me by rapping on the window so hard I think she's going to break it. "You could just turn the door handle," I tell her.

"Are you kidding me? A place like this probably has an alarm on every door that's not the front door."

"Only the windows," I joke, but I have no idea.

"For real?"

I look a little closer. "Looks like they have security cameras up outside," I say as I point to the top corner of the massive roof. I reach around her and grab the doorknob. My arm touches her shoulder. She doesn't move away. I can't believe how happy I feel.

The door flies open. Sam's face is in our faces. Barf. "Hey, you sneakin' in the back, Venus," he says.

"Charlie and I were just parking," she answers.

His face is filled with confusion. "The car. We were just parking the car," she repeats. What is that about?

"I have someone to do that," he answers before sticking the red cup he holds between his teeth and holding it there.

"I know that, but mom's kind of particular about the car, so I thought I should park it myself," Venus says. I feel strange when I realize she could have told him my thing about parking, but she didn't. What does that mean? Is she embarrassed by me?

"Actually," I start to say, but she claps a hand over my mouth. This is weird.

"So, what you drinking, Sam, and where can we get some?"

she asks in a voice I don't like. At least not when she's using it on him.

He takes the cup from his mouth and holds it out. "It's a white claw cocktail," he says. "Wanna try mine?"

"No thanks. I'll just take some wine from a box," she answers in a less friendly voice. "You got any of that?"

Sam blinks a few times. "Whatever we have is in here. Help yourself. I gotta get back to beer pong. See you later."

"Yeah, okay," Venus says before turning back to me. "So what do you want to drink?"

"I usually have a juice box," I say, because that's the last thing I drank when I was at his house.

"Juicebox," some guy blares in my ear. Where did he come from? "This guy wants a—"

Venus punches this guy in the gut. Her hand is around the back of his neck. Her lips are near his ear. What is she doing?

He nods and limps away. "Psycho bitch," he says from across the room.

Venus salutes him and turns back to me. "How about we find something to pour into a cup," she says with a smile so nice I can't believe she just punched someone. "I gotta find some ice for my hand," she adds while pouring me something.

"I'm sorry," I tell her.

"Don't worry about it. He's a tool."

Creed appears out of nowhere. She grabs Venus by the hand. "C'mon! Come dance with me!"

I nudge Venus. "Go ahead, go have fun. I'm just going to hang out," I tell her, and I do, for all of five minutes before the noise and the crowd gets to me, and I feel like I can't breathe. I creep up the stairs to Charlie's room to climb out his window onto the roof like we did when we were kids. The music is still too loud, but at least it doesn't hurt my ears like it did when I was inside.

Venus hit a guy because he was rude to me. Why would she do that if she didn't kind of like me? Did she hit him because he's a jerk, or was it more than that? I wish I could have been the one to hit him, but then he would have hit me back, and that would have been disastrous. I don't know the first thing about fighting. I don't know if I could hit someone at all. Like maybe if I had a harpoon. I could throw it at him. Or I could beat him with a fishing rod. I need my hands for drawing though, so it would be stupid of me to hit him with my fist. The thought of not being able to draw makes me feel sick to my stomach. I should stop thinking about that.

I lay back on the roof and stare at the sky and think about Venus, even though I don't want to. What if she meets someone here tonight, and she decides she likes them? What if Sam keeps talking to her and she starts listening to what he says? Sam always knows what to say to girls. Words just come out, and they're always the right ones and they always make him look so smart and so funny and so perfect to whatever girl he's talking to. Words come out of my mouth and girls run away, because no girl wants to hear about how many different species of clown fish there are in the South East Pacific, but that's like all I talk about. Ocean life is fascinating just like the fact that Cinnamon Clownfish are so similar to Tomato Clownfish; the two are often confused unless the person knows that Cinnamon Clownfish have a wider head-band and black fins.

Movement in Sam's room catches the corner of my eye. It's Creed. What the heck is she doing in his room? I scoot over to the window and open it. "Creed," I whisper shout as I stick my head in the window.

Her blue eyes bug. "What are you doing out there?" she hisses back.

"What are you doing in there," I say just as the doorknob to his room starts to turn.

"Oh, shit," she says before hanging halfway out the window and scrambling onto the roof beside me. She closes the window before shoving me up backward until I can't see in his room. She's in front of me. "Shhh," she says.

"Who's in his room?" I ask.

"He is," she tells me.

"Was he coming up there to see you?" I ask, even though I don't want to.

Creed is quiet for way too long. "No," she whimpers. "Apparently he is coming up there to see Venus."

I think she's crying, and I hate that I don't know what to do. I'm terrible with girls crying, especially right now, because I want to cry.

"What are they doing."

Creed ducks and doesn't answer me. I hate this. I want to look in the window, but I don't want to. Because if I look in the window and Venus is dancing with Sam, or kissing Sam, or smiling at Sam, I'll know that the one thing I am most afraid of is happening. Venus may have kissed me, but she doesn't think I'm all that special. She doesn't see me as *the guy*, she sees me like she sees every other guy.

My gut tightens. My hands sweat. My head feels like it's going to explode. I want to peek through that window. I cannot bear to look inside. What's inside could be the end of the relationship between me and Venus. This is a total nightmare.

"Creed," I whisper.

"What," she moans.

"What are they doing?"

"I don't know, Charlie. Just shut up. You're such an asshole."

I've never had Creed call me that before. I don't think I like it. I take out my phone. I will message her and see how long it takes her to answer me. I open my Snapchat and find her name, but then I stop. What could I possibly say that needs to be said right now? "Are you ready to go home," I say to Creed.

She doesn't answer. I scoot closer to her. "Are you ready to go home," I repeat.

"I don't want to go home, but I don't want to be here either," she says. "I hate high school, and I hate Sam Birk, and I hate his stupid party. Guys are so freaking stupid," she whines, but I don't mind. She's right. Guys are pretty stupid. At least when it comes to girls. And I am no exception. Sam is someone I hate right now too. And high school sucks. Big time. Just like this party.

"So you want to leave?" I ask while trying not to sound too hopeful. If I want something too much, she will take great joy in not giving it to me. Creed can be a real turd.

"Yeah. Probably."

I get back on my phone and Snap Venus. "Creed and I are ready to leave whenever you are."

"Where are you," she Snaps me five minutes later. "I've been looking for you."

"Venus is looking for me," I tell Creed.

"Well good for you," she pops off.

"Do you think we should go back inside, or should I tell her we're sitting on the roof outside Sam's room?"

Creed turns around and punches me in my toe. "No. You should definitely not tell her we are lurking outside his window."

"Then what do I tell her?"

"Tell her nothing. She was in his bedroom. She knows how I feel about him. I can't believe she would do this to me," she says in between sobbing and trying to breathe. Her shoulders move up and down.

"I have to tell her something," I say.

"Put your phone away. We have to go find another window to climb back through," she says. It's not the best idea, but it's not the worst, and I have no suggestions. Plus, I'm relieved for something to do. Maybe if Creed gets up and moves around, she will stop crying. We stumble around on Sam's roof like a couple of drunks.

"I need my phone light," I tell her, just about the time I turn my ankle and fall down hard. My shin hits something sharp. It stings. "Creed. I fell down," I say.

"You're such a klutz," she tells me as she comes over to where I am. Her phone light comes on. "Oh, crap. You're bleeding," she says. "It might be bad."

I clutch my pant leg and hold it tight to my leg. "Sit down," I tell her, because I know that voice. She's about to pass out on me. "You can't faint on top of a roof," I tell her just as she slumps to one side. She falls with a thud. We are officially the worst partygoers. I don't know what to do, but my pant leg is kind of wet. I don't think that's a good sign. Mom's going to be so mad at me for bleeding on my new jeans. "Please get Sam and find me on the roof," I type to Venus. "I think I hurt myself."

"You are on the roof," Venus answers.

"I'm bleeding," I reply.

Seven minutes later, Sam and Venus find us. Venus has a box in her hands. "It's a first aid kit. Let me see your leg," she orders.

I tug up my pant leg. Sam makes a gagging sound. "Dude. You know how I feel about blood."

"Look the other way but keep the light on his leg," Venus says. "I need to see what I'm doing."

Sam bumps my hand with his phone. "Here take it. I can't. I'm sorry, but I can't." He looks past me at Creed, who is unusually quiet. "You want to go somewhere else," he says.

"Sure," she answers. "But only because I don't like blood either."

Whatever Venus pours on my leg stings. So bad. It feels like she sent fire up my leg, but I don't say anything. I just hold my breath and wait for it to go away. Her hand is on my arm. "Are you okay?"

"Yeah. It stings a little. That's all," I answer.

"That means it stings like a mother," Creed calls from somewhere else on the roof.

Venus waves her hands over my leg. "I'm sorry. I was cleaning it. I don't want it to get infected. Do you know when your last tetanus shot was?"

"No," I say.

"Well, you better call the nurse about it and figure it out." She squeezes a tube. "This is just ointment. It should not hurt," she says before she smears it all over my leg. "Now I'm going to put dressings on your leg and then I'm going to wrap it," she says.

"What are you, like a Girl Scout?" I ask to keep my mind off the pain. Mostly.

"No. I was a junior paramedic in training. So what?" Venus mumbles before putting the dressings on my leg and wrapping them with gauze. Her hands fly around my leg like an expert. She is so cool.

"So are you all gonna ditch my party?" Sam asks from somewhere behind us. He actually sounds like he cares.

"We thought about it," Creed answers. I think she stands beside him.

"What can I do to make you stay?" he asks as we trail along behind him.

"Bring us food in your room," Venus replies, being the last person to step through his window.

"What do you want?"

"Surprise us," she tells him.

"Creed, you want to come with?" Sam asks.

Venus grabs her by the arm. "No, I need her to stay here. With me. I have something to tell her."

Creed looks torn between going with Sam and staying with Venus, but Venus keeps her hold on my sister's wrist. Sam gives us all one last look. "Fine. I'll be back."

The door closes behind him. Creed whips around to look at Venus. "What are you doing? I wanted to go with him."

Venus rolls her eyes. "If you go with him, you won't have time to look around while he's not here." Then she takes one of Creed's earrings out of her ear.

Creed's hand flies to her ear. "What are you doing?"

Venus holds it up in front of her. "If you leave it here, you'll have a reason to talk to him about it later."

Creed's face breaks out into a full-out grin. "You're so devious."

Venus wrinkles her nose. "I'm going to pretend I didn't hear that word. It's kind of cringe."

"Is it," Creed says in an even weirder voice than before.

"Just hurry up and get your butt moving around the room," Venus says. Girls are so weird.

"Did you look at my room when I wasn't in it?" I ask Venus when the thought occurs to me.

"Yeah, she totally did," Creed answers before Venus opens her mouth. "That was before I knew she liked you. Trust me, I would not have let her go in your room if I had known," Creed says as she floats around Sam's room checking out his framed baseball card collection, his three books on the shelf, and his posters on the wall with quotes on them about being the best you can be. Venus glances around a little as well. I want to ask her what she was doing up here before, but I don't know if I want the answer.

She flies past me, bumping my shoulder with hers. She lifts something from behind the lamp on his night table. "Is this you?" she asks. I force myself to stop staring at her beautiful face that I could stare at forever.

I can't believe Sam still has that picture of me and him at a field day in second grade. His arm is around my shoulders. We're staring into the camera with goofy grins on our faces while we both hold up our hands in the shape of an L for loser, because we got last place in the three-legged race when I tripped, and we both went down. Sam was so mad. He hates losing. He always has, even when he was seven. I felt so terrible for making him fall, but he never said anything to me about it. We were never partners again though.

So we were walking away, but we didn't walk fast enough to outrun stupid Garrett and Brent as they called us losers, so when Mom came over with her camera to take a photo of the one and only time I was in a sporting event with Sam, he turned to me with a grin and a big L shaped with his fingers. "Loser," he joked. A sense of relief came over me and I laughed as I mimicked him.

"Sam and Charlie, look at me!" Mom ordered, and so we did, with our big L's stuck to our foreheads as we laughed some more. "You boys are so silly," she scolded, but I could tell she was happy too. That was a good day.

I reorient to find Venus watching me. "Yeah, that's me," I say.

Venus puts the photo back in its place. Creed grabs her by the arm. "What were you doing in here with Sam?"

"Not what you think," Venus answers. Then the door flies open.

"I'm back," Sam chirps. "And I brought sustenance."

He lays the huge plate of food on his bed. Venus and Creed crowd him. "Only you would have bacon-wrapped lobster tail at a high school beer party," Venus tells him, but it doesn't sound like a compliment.

Sam gives her a strange look. "If you don't like my food, I can take it back to the kitchen."

Venus grabs something off the plate and pops it in her mouth. "I didn't say I didn't like it. I'm just saying it's kinda extra."

Creed looks up at Sam from where she sits beside the plate full of food. "I think it all looks delicious. Thank you for bringing it up here."

Sam pulls a plate from the paper bag he's holding and holds it out to me. "Here. I brought you a plate so you can put whatever food on there and it won't be touching."

I walk over and take it from him. "Thanks."

He turns on the huge flat-screen television mounted on the wall. "Now. Who wants to watch the party going on downstairs?"

Venus chokes a little on her food. She turns away from all of us. "Are you for real," Creed says. "You can do that?"

He nods as four screens come up on the one big screen. It's so weird seeing our classmates interact with each other. "Is that Charming sucking face with Bates? I thought he was with Kara," Creed says.

"Yeah, I don't know," Sam answers as they both step closer to the screen.

"Maybe we should watch something else," Venus says. "This is too weird."

Creed whips around to look at her. "It's not weird. Besides, who am I going to tell? No one listens to me. No one even notices me."

Venus's hand is on her hip. Her other hand points at the screen. "So if you were sucking face with some guy downstairs, you wouldn't care if we were sitting up here watching you like a bunch of creepers," she accuses.

Creed looks a little less sure of herself. "First of all, I wouldn't be doing that in front of everyone. That's just gross. And secondly, I wouldn't be doing that unless it was..." she stops talking.

"Turn it off," Venus says in a loud voice.

Sam flips the channel to something else. "How about we watch a movie instead," he says.

"But this is your party," Creed tells him. "Don't you want to be down there with everyone?"

"Nah. It's alright. I've had three other parties before this one. They're all the same. Trust me, no one notices that I'm not down there, but I'm okay with it." He looks over at me. "Charlie's up here, so you know. I want to be up here too."

"I'm sorry I'm ruining your good time," I tell him in the middle of picking out things to put on my plate.

"You're not," Sam says. "Really. It's cool."

Venus looks at him and then at me. "So, Sam. Tell me a Charlie and Sam story and make it good."

Sam laughs out loud. "Wanna hear about the time I took Charlie to watch my favorite baseball team at the big stadium?"

Ugh. I know what's coming. I spent most of that day in the hallway near the concession stand. It wasn't my fault someone painted a terrible mural of Marlins, even though they were the opposing team and the artist got most of it wrong. Everyone knows Marlins don't wear sunglasses or hats, and that was just the start of what was wrong with the rest of it.

"So the Marlins are like my all-time favorite team, even though I've never been to Florida, and even though I've lived here my whole life. So, like they were going to be playing here, and my dad told me he would take me to a game, and so I asked Charlie, because I know he likes fish from the ocean or whatever, and I thought the fact that I was inviting him to a game with a team named after a fish would help him forgive me for making him sit in the crowd all afternoon," Sam says with a grin.

"I'm guessing it didn't," Venus comments in a voice that sounds like she's about to laugh.

"Um, no. It did not. Charlie spent the majority of the game staring at the newly-painted mural that was such a big deal it even made the local paper, but it was not good enough for Charlie, the future marine biologist, even though he was only nine years old."

"I'm sorry I ruined your day at the ballpark," I tell Sam while wishing I could mean it. .

"You were nine and you already knew everything there is to know about a Marlin," Venus adds, but she doesn't sound annoyed or cast me as a freak. She sounds like she's proud of me. I don't know what to say.

"I really like fish."

TWENTY-TWO

Venus

Listening to Sam tell stories about him and Charlie when they were boys, cracks me up, but it also makes me a little sad for Charlie. He clearly loves the ocean, and he doesn't understand why other people don't. He takes it all so seriously. It's a good thing he's so focused he doesn't seem to care that other people find his fixation on the ocean and all the fish in it more than a little strange. Although I find it hard to understand, I hope someday I find something that interests me as much as marine biology interests him.

"I have no idea what I want to be when I grow up," I say in between stories.

Creed leans into me. "I don't either, but that's okay. We're young. We've got two more years before we go to college."

"You'd better figure out where you're going, Creed. College takes lots of preparation," Charlie warns.

She snorts. "Only if you want to get into a brainiac school like the ones in California. The rest of us are just happy to be admitted."

Sam makes a face at her while nudging her hip with his foot. "Whatever, Creed. It's not like your parents can't pay for his college tuition."

I'm so confused. "Seriously, spoiled little rich boy who lives in a fricking mansion? You're going to give him crap about his parents having money?"

Sam levels me with a look. "What's with you getting so defensive over Charlie? Mr. Smarty Pants can speak for himself."

"But he won't, because you're his best friend, so it doesn't matter what you say about him, or how much crap you say, he's going to keep his mouth shut, but that doesn't mean I have to," I spout, even though I know I should keep quiet. My face heats as fast as my anger rises. I hate bullies, and in my opinion, Sam is a bully.

"And there's nothing wrong with having goals or working toward paying your own way as much as you can," I add. "My mom is a single mother, but that doesn't mean I plan on getting a bunch of money just because of it. She works her butt off, and she's a successful career woman. I don't expect her to apologize for it."

"Girl, chill," Creed says with a smile, but I hear the tension in her voice. "No one said anything bad about your mom."

"She's probably single because she's as cold as Hilary Clinton or something," Sam mutters. I can tell by his smirk he knows he's pushing my buttons. And dammit if it doesn't work.

"For your information, my father left my mother because he couldn't take the fact that she was better at her job than he was at his. It threatened him as a man. He tried to hold her back. He tried to control her. She got tired of it and she left. When she did, she took me with her. I'm proud of my mother and all she has accomplished."

Sam looks uncertain, but I can tell he has more to say. "Maybe that's just how you see it because you're a girl."

I can't believe he's so stupid. "Maybe you can't hear what I'm saying because you're a guy."

"That's sexist," he says, but I can tell he's not sure about it.

"What's sexist is my mother having to hide her success or apologize for it because she's a female. If she were a man, no one would say anything. They'd be too busy praising her and patting her on the back." I point a finger in his face. "The point

I'm making is some men can't stand to watch a woman climb the corporate ladder in a skirt because they're too busy trying to look up it. If a woman puts on a pair of pants and climbs the same ladder they climb, they say stupid, demeaning things that aren't even true." I stare him down and try to remind myself he's no different than any other small-minded guy I've ever met, but he's sitting right in front of me, and he's not getting it. "Do you think anyone would have made sexual jokes about Kamala Harris getting to where she is if she were a man? Have you ever heard someone say a man slept his way to the top? No. They would never say that about a man who has a position of power, but they will say it about a woman. It's such a double standard."

Sam blinks a few times. I can tell he still doesn't agree with me, but he's also not going to say anything. We sit here and continue to stare awkwardly at each other. I'm not going to be the first one to look away since I'm right.

"Did you know the female praying mantis will eat the male after they mate?" Charlie asks.

"And yet the male will walk into her trap every time," Sam comments.

"Actually, they only walk in once," Creed corrects him. And then she freezes, as if she's afraid she went too far.

We all freeze, but then Sam's hand goes to his face, covering his mouth. His shoulders shake. He's laughing, and then I'm laughing.

"I didn't mean to be funny," Charlie says, and then we laugh even harder. "I was merely pointing out that in some ecosystems, the woman dominates because she's a cannibal."

It's so gruesome to think about. I don't know why his graphic description makes me laugh even more, but it does. I laugh so hard I tip over sideways and bump into Creed. My head flops on her leg and I stare at her. "Your brother is a trip," I say.

"I know," she answers in between her laughing. "He might even need stitches."

Her statement sobers me right up. I'm so horrible. I can't

believe I forgot about his leg injury so quickly. I look over at him. "Charlie, is your leg hurting?"

"If you're asking if it's throbbing, then yes, it hurts."

I feel like the worst friend ever. "I'm so sorry. We should get you to the hospital." I look back at Sam. "I'm sorry, but I think he needs to go."

Sam studies me for half a second. "I think you're right." He gets to his feet before grabbing Charlie under the arm on the opposite side of his injury. "Come on, then. Let's get you to the hospital."

Creed's eyes widen. "You're going with us?"

"Um, yeah. The dude fell on my roof. I think it's only fair I tag along," Sam says. "In fact, I'll drive you. There's no sense in making Charlie walk through all those cars, and finding Venus's car will take twice as long."

I consider his advice. "Why don't you take Charlie, and Creed and I will catch up to you," I suggest. "I bet his parents will want to meet us at the hospital once they realize he's there."

"Don't worry, Sam," Creed says as we walk along behind them down the steps. "My parents love you, they won't be mad."

"I can't believe I fell on your throwing star," Charlie says to Sam when we get to the garage.

"Yeah. I can't believe you found it. I thought it was long gone," Sam answers.

"Why in the heck did you have a throwing star?" Creed asks while she hangs on Charlie's door.

"Because they're cool," the guys say in unison and then Charlie shuts the door. Creed and I stay where we are while Sam backs out of the garage. We walk out into the lines of cars. It's so strange to think this is someone's backyard.

"What do Sam's parents do?" I ask Creed on the way to my car.

"We don't really talk about it," she answers. "It's all part of the cool mystery that surrounds Sam Birk's life," she says in a dramatic tone.

"That's weird," I tell her once we're in the car.

"It's not weird, it's eccentric," she argues. "You know, because he has a shit ton of money."

I drive out of the line of cars and go toward the house before spying the cement pathway leading around to the front. "So why were you in Sam's bedroom?" Creed asks, and I know she isn't talking about just a minute ago.

"Don't get all mad at me," I say. I'm actually relieved she saw me and that she asked, because I've been trying to figure out how to tell her ever since it happened. "So I was dancing, okay. You know, because you were there."

"Yeah, until I got thirsty and went to get a drink and when I got back you were like gone," she accuses, but she's right. That's exactly what happened. Well, mostly. I mean, Sam Birk, the ever-present opportunist, happened. As soon as it was just the two of us, he grabbed my hand and tugged me through the dancers. I knew where we were probably going, and that he was leading me away from Creed, but I was also a tad bit annoyed with her for leaving me alone with him. She had to know what he would try. Like the worst kind of friend, I followed him upstairs to his room. We were barely inside when he made a move on me. He was so smooth about it too. He was all, "I'm sorry but I just needed to get you alone to talk about something." He looked truly concerned.

So I was like *what* and then he stepped into my space. I thought I knew everything there was to know about Sam Birk, like how he's always so confident and cool. How his cheesy smile with just enough mischief to make you wonder what he's up to never stops. How he always looks so sure of himself no matter where he is or what he's doing. He just has this charm that draws people to him. He can't help it. And when all of that was centered on me, it was too much. When his hand went around my waist, and he pulled me in, I went. And when he dipped his head to kiss me, I went along with that too. I got lost in being kissed by Sam Birk, so lost I didn't notice how fast he was moving until he'd unhooked my bra. I came back to myself real quick. My first instinct was to shove him away, but he was too solid. So when he didn't move, I fell over backward on my butt.

He'd laughed and put out his hand. "I've never had a girl literally fall at my feet before," he teased, and I knew. I knew I could just giggle and relish in his clever little comeback, and pick up where we left off. I could get lost all over again in his kiss, and forget about Charlie and Creed and how hurt they would be that I had betrayed them both for some time in a room alone with Sam, the hottest guy at Seeberger High. But my thoughts returned to Creed. She would be devastated. It might very well be the end of our friendship. I felt so dumb. Was losing Creed worth having a little fun with Sam?

And what about Charlie? Would he forgive me? Would he ever see me the same if I hooked up with his best friend? And what about me? Would I still see myself the same if I chose Sam over Charlie and my best friend? Could I really do what he was asking me to do? I forced myself to look up at him. "We should not be doing this," I said.

"What are we doing," he'd said in his flirty, light-hearted manner. His look of total bewilderment made me think we'd just been sitting there playing cards.

"You know what I mean, Sam. Don't be that way."

He gave me another look. "I'm simply being who I am," he argued.

"You know how she feels about you, and you know how he feels about me," I'd argued. "But please don't tell her I said any of this."

His flirty face turned a little mean. "You mean don't tell her that you kissed me," he'd said.

I was so flustered and so angry. "I didn't kiss you. You kissed me," I argued. "I should know. I was here."

"There's something between us, Venus. If you have to fall down to get away from me, I'd have to be stupid not to notice."

He was right. About all of it. "It's not my fault you're who you are," I said. "So many girls want you, so choose one of them. Why do you want to be with me?"

He rolled his eyes before sitting down on the edge of his bed. "If you're ignoring me or pushing me away to make me want you more, it's working."

"Trust me, that's so no not what I'm doing," I said, and I mostly believed it.

"It's not?"

"No. I came up here because you lead me out of the room and up the stairs. You had a hold of my hand. I wasn't about to make a scene downstairs on the middle of the dance floor. Did you really want me to reject you in front of everyone at your own party," I challenged.

"If you didn't want to be here with me right now, you would have," he said as he maintained eye contact while basically calling me a liar, and I hated myself because I knew that he was right. And then I hated him for making me feel as low as he could just to get with me, and that's when I snapped.

"Do you really want to betray your best friend and my best friend to have a little fun with me," I said. "Because we both know whatever happens right here in this room won't go further than tonight. We both know what type of guy you are. You don't care about anything but getting in a girl's pants," I spat the words at him. "We both know if you were a girl, everyone would call you a *slut*, but since you're a guy your behavior makes you cool."

He recoiled, as if I had slapped him. "You're crazy."

"Am I?" I asked. "Are you telling me if something happens between us and your guy friends find out, they won't be high-fiving you and calling you the man while smearing my name in the same sentence?"

"I wouldn't tell," he said in a low voice. "It'd be our little secret."

My stomach churned at his words. "If you're trying to be sexy, that's so not," I said. "That's just disgusting."

"I can't believe I invited you to my party," he pouted.

"I can't believe you think waving your popularity in my face is going to get you some," I retorted.

"Do you have to talk like that?" he said.

"Are you telling me that's not what you're after," I replied, as I glared at him. "Or was this just a loyalty test? Were you just seeing how far I would go with you to know if I was really interested in Charlie," I said, throwing him a bone.

"Yes," he said with a big nod. "That's totally what I was doing."

I gave him a look that I hoped told him he was so full of crap, but I wasn't going to call him on it, for Charlie's sake. "That's what I thought," I said as I got up and walked across the room to open his bedroom door. "Let's just keep this little loyalty secret between us, shall we? I would hate to have to tell Charlie about your bad behavior, or how far you were willing to go for a *friend*," I said in the meanest voice I could manage before exiting the room.

"So what happened in his room?" she demands in between giving me directions to the nearest hospital.

"I, um, well, I followed him off the dance floor and up the stairs because he told me he wanted to show me something, and so I went. So we went into his room and he sort of like hugged me, and then we kissed, and then I told him I wasn't interested in him that way, and he said he was just testing me to see if I was serious about liking Charlie." I clear my throat. "So please don't tell your brother. There's no need for him to know. It would just hurt his feelings unnecessarily."

She giggles. That was the last response I thought I would get. "I can't believe Sam would kiss you just to see if you like Charlie. That's so over-the-top. He's so dramatic." She swats at my arm. "So how was it? Was it like totally hot? I bet it was. I bet he was. I bet it was hard to remember your first name after Sam kissed you." She sighs. "I hate that you kissed Sam before I did, but I forgive you. I understand why it was so hard not to kiss him. He's just so friggin' hot."

"Thanks," I tell her as we pull into the hospital parking lot. "I hope I wrapped your brother's leg right. I felt so bad making his leg hurt worse, but I didn't want it to get infected."

"Relax, Venus. You did more than Sam or I could ever do. You helped stop the bleeding, and you didn't freak out. That's huge."

I hear her words, and I know she means them, but I feel like the worst kind of friend. Word vomit pours out of me. "I wanted to kiss him, okay. Like there was a part of me that was flattered that he chose to take me to his bedroom. And you're right about Sam. There's just something about him that is so hot. Maybe it's because he's popular. Maybe it's because when he smiles at you, you forget anyone else is in the room. Maybe it's because he has a gift for making you feel like you are the only girl he's ever thought about in that way. I don't know. But I wanted to kiss him. I wanted to know what it would be like, and I'm sorry," I say. And I mean every word. "But once we kissed, I knew. I knew your friendship meant more to me than anything I could have done with Sam. I knew that the idea of maybe being Charlie's girlfriend one day meant more to me than one night in Sam's room, and so I told Sam that. I told him I didn't want to kiss him or anything else, and that I knew whatever he intended to do with me tonight wouldn't last more than that moment in his room."

I stare at my hands in my lap. I can't believe I spilled all of that in the car between us. "You said all that to Sam Birk," Creed says after the longest time.

"I did," I say.

"You're such a badass," she says. "You're like totally my hero."

I look over at her. "Thanks, but I don't feel like a hero. I feel kind of stupid for ever going to his room in the first place."

She shrugs. "Well. Maybe I'll kiss him someday, and maybe I won't." She takes my hand in hers. "But you and me? We're friends for life. You're my ride or die, bee-yotch."

I giggle. I can't help it. "Thanks. You're not too bad yourself." I glance at my watch. "Can we go inside now and see your brother?"

"Yeah, but you know Charlie can handle it on his own, right? He's eighteen. Technically he's of the age to give consent for his own medical treatment."

I giggle again. "Yeah, right. Like your brother knows anything about being on his own. He doesn't even know how to drive a car."

She opens the car door. "You don't have to be so mean. Where he's going they have public transportation."

I giggle. "He still has to figure out bus routes and how to pay," I say as I follow her inside. "I'm just saying."

She doesn't answer because she's on her phone. We're barely inside the ER when Sam comes through the double doors. "Sorry, Creed, but he only wants to see Venus."

TWENTY-THREE

Charlie

"Dude," Sam said to me while holding out his phone. "Check this out. You're blowing up social media because you fell on top of my roof." He shook his head as he stood near the head of my bed so he couldn't see what they were doing with my lower leg and ankle. "That's wild. People are saying you're suicidal and that you were flirting with death as you stood near the edge." He studied me carefully. "Were you, man? Were you trying to hurt yourself, because that's not cool, man. I will go to therapy with you. If you need therapy, I will go. "

His words were so weird. "No. I don't need therapy," I said. *I just need you to quit kissing the one girl I like*, I thought, but I couldn't get the words to come out of my mouth.

"Okay, but you should know man, because we're like best friends and all that, that I kissed her tonight, and I guess I thought I better tell you, so things don't get weird between us or whatever."

That was funny he would say that, because now things are weird between us. Super weird. I don't want them to be, but all I can't think of is her dancing with him and letting him get close, just like she did to me. I can't believe Venus would do this to me. Why didn't she say something about it?

"Your sister's here. I'm just gonna go get her."

"I want to talk to Venus," I blurted, though I wasn't sure why.

"That's cool," he said before he practically ran out of the ER room.

And now Venus is here, standing by my bedside, looking all concerned. I wish I knew why she kissed him. "I know you kissed Sam," I begin. The words flow out of me, even though I don't want them to.

"I did," she confirms.

"Why?" I ask, because I have to know.

"I wanted to know what it would be like to kiss Sam Birk." As if that's an acceptable answer for tearing my heart to shreds. I glance up at the monitor. How can my pulse rate be 84 when it feels like it should be flatlined? I don't think these machines are working.

"Was it everything you wanted it to be?" I'm not sure what passing a kidney stone feels like, although I've been told it's akin to peeing out a cocklebur. I feel as though I have one in my throat, floating around, poking things I don't want poked. Almost-having-a-girlfriend is absolute misery.

"I think so," she says before putting her hand on her forehead. "I'm sorry, Charlie. I'm not saying anything very well."

I don't know what she's talking about. "I think you're saying it quite well," I reply. "I have no doubts that kissing Sam Birk was as pleasant as you hoped for. I'm sure you two will be very happy together."

She giggles. I can't believe she's being so cruel. To my face. While I'm lying in a hospital bed. "You know Sam," she says, and then three people walk into the room.

"Okay, Charlie. We're going to take you back to x-ray now just to be sure there's nothing broken. We can't have you bearing weight and causing further injury to that sore ankle."

"I'm pretty sure I wouldn't feel it," I answer them. "Other parts of me hurt much worse," I say as I look back at Venus, who sits down in the chair. She watches as they wheel me in my bed out of the room.

Fortunately, I don't have to get out of my bed for them to x-ray my lower leg, ankle, and foot. Thoughts whirl around inside my head. *What did she mean by telling me I know Sam? Is she trying to tell me she's fallen for him already, and that's just too bad for me? Is she telling me Sam is a terrific kisser? Is that why she said it? Is she saying she and Sam will be together or not? Why would she leave me hanging like that? How am I going to go to school every day and watch her holding hands with Sam, smiling her special smile at him, catch him kissing her at his locker which is just seven lockers from mine? Is there any way I can spend the rest of my school year at home online? Maybe I can claim severe duress. Maybe I can get back into Mr. J's classroom and out of Spanish III. Maybe I can go to Spain and finish the rest of my Senior year as a foreign exchange student.*

"Alright, Charlie. We are all done with you. It's time to go back to your room and wait for the results."

"I already know the results. She doesn't want to be with me," I say.

"What's that?" the friendly man in scrubs asks.

"Nothing." I can't believe I'm talking about my nonexistent love life to a guy who works in the ER. I've officially gone insane.

"Well," she says once the room is empty. "How'd it go?"

"I don't know," I say. "It's a wait-and-see kind of thing."

"So you're on hold?" she asks with a silly smile on her face. What's that about?

"Yeah, I guess you could say that."

She steps a little closer to the side of my bed. "Waiting can be very difficult. Trust me, I would know."

"Okay," I say. I have no idea what she's saying.

"Charlie," she says.

"What."

"I have something very important to tell you, and I need you to listen to me."

She's going to tell me how much she likes Sam, and that they were meant to be together, and that's she so sorry, but that's just the way it is. And then I'm going to keep my mouth shut even though I know he's going to break her heart, just like so many other girls at our high school who think they're going to be like the magical unicorn that captures Sam's short attention span. He's my best friend, but he's kind of a jerk. Once he gets what he wants from a girl, he loses interest, and he dumps her. That's just who he is. I just can't believe she fell for him. There must be something magical that goes on in his bedroom.

"You're not listening." Her voice cuts through the incoming scenario that I want no part of playing itself over and over in my head. She likes Sam. There's nothing I can do about it. I saw them kissing. I know what I saw.

"I like you, Charlie Barren," she says, and that's it. I don't want her to say any more things. Ever again. Except those five words a few more times.

"You like me," I repeat like a broken record.

"Did you not hear what I just said," she teases, but I'm not laughing. This is serious. The girl of my dreams just told me she likes *me,* and not in a platonic way.

"3,895 words plus five."

"Excuse me?"

"That's how many words you've spoken to me since the day we met," I tell her, even though I'm pretty sure I sound a little crazy.

"And you know this how?" she asks, but at least she doesn't look at me like she thinks I'm lying.

"Because I counted them. In my head." *Duh. How else would I know?*

"Do you keep a running tally of everyone words? I can't decide if that's freaking amazing or just really weird."

I can't believe I told her this. Why can't I just blow it off and say I made it up and I have no idea how many words she's told me like any normal guy would do? Because I'm not normal. I'm me. "I, um. I only count your words, and that number might not be exact, because my head got a little muddled when we kissed, so I may have forgotten a few here and there. And it's hard for me to differentiate between the words you actually say and the ones I hear in my head when you're near me, so."

She gazes into my eyes. Her cheeks turn pink. She shifts from one foot to the other. Her hands fidget with each other. I think I said too much, but once I started talking, I couldn't stop. Grandpa always said to go for broke when it counts, and I never really knew what that meant, but I think I know now.

"Charlie," she says as her hand touches mine.

"Yeah."

"Did they put you under back there?"

Her words confuse me. I wasn't gone long enough to be put under. "They didn't, but you do."

Her tiny smile grows. She waits an unbearable amount of time. Her thumb draws shapes on the back of my hand. I never want it to stop. "I guess I just have one thing to say,' she says before clearing her throat. "In our future interactions, I hope the 'plus five' are the ones you hold onto."

I thread my fingers through hers and still her busy thumb. "I can do that, so long as you hold my hand."

She looks at me with the sweetest smile. "I will. I wouldn't want you to fall. I only have so many first aid kits."

I look at our hands before looking up at her. "I've already fallen, Venus, and I intend to keep falling, so long as you catch me."

Her green eyes burn bright as she leans over me. "What am I going to do with you, biology boy?"

I give her hand a squeeze. "You could keep me. There aren't too many of my kind left in the species."

Her lips touch mine. It's perfection. "Charlie Barren, people can't be classified, and you are one of a kind."

I disagree, but I keep my mouth shut. Kissing runs a close second to classifying the species. Second place feels pretty good.

I Can't Unknow

It would be easier if I
    Didn't know the way
    Expectation lights
    Your face every
    Morning

As if you don't see
    You're walking into
    My abyss – a
    Building filled with
    Chaos

Obnoxious laughter
    Burns my ears.
    Words fly as fast
    As swinging arms
    And hands

Reminders it is
    Me who is
    Out of place

In a clockwork of
Salinity

I wade unwillingly
Through throngs
Of chattering
Joyful mouths,
Wishing

For silence and
The rough brush
Of the familiar
Dry, unforgiving
Green stalks

As they rise
From my beloved
Freshwater space
Scraping my wrists
Unsettling me

Until I met you.
The heat of your
Hands, the draw of
Your eyes full of
Promises

Before I met you
I didn't know I
Was drowning
I didn't know I
Hadn't surfaced

You regulate
My anxiety-induced

Anoxia that steals
My functionality.
You are my
Operculum.

THANK YOU FOR READING

* * *

Did you enjoy this book?

We invite you to leave a review at your favorite book site, such as Goodreads, Amazon, Barnes & Noble, etc.

DID YOU KNOW THAT LEAVING A REVIEW...

- Helps other readers find books they may enjoy.
- Gives you a chance to let your voice be heard.
- Gives authors recognition for their hard work.
- Doesn't have to be long. A sentence or two about why you liked the book will do.

About the Author

I live in the beautiful Flint Hills of Kansas. I'm blessed to do two things I love- nursing and writ ing. I have wonderful family support including my husband, our son, daughter-in-law, and two daughters, my parents and in-laws, and too many more to mention as well as many friends who willingly give their input whenever it is requested. I'm thankful for the characters and stories as they come along, as well as the companies who publish them and the readers who read them.

facebook.com/RachelAnneJonesAuthor

x.com/Jones1974Ra

instagram.com/diari197

tiktok.com/@idreamofdandelions

Also by Rachel Anne Jones

With Fire & Ice YA Books
Novels

Marmalade Uncapped

Essence of Emma

Lovestruck: Kisses, Lies & Oatmeal Cream Pies

Ramblin' Nash: A Day in the Life of a Flower Shop Boy

Biology Boy Love

All Or Nothing Series

Chasing Denver

Rough Terrain

A Firm Plateau

Radioactive Series

Love and Armageddon

House of Cinders

M.I.A.

The X-Factor

* * *

With Satin Romance

A Joy-Filled Christmas

Pickles-N-Fries and Fireflies

Stealing the Glass Slipper

A Stolen Heart